THE PARROT GREEN SAREE

NABANEETA DEV SEN

TRANSLATED FROM BENGALI BY

TUTUN MUKHERJEE

THORNBIRD

NIYOGI BOOKS

Published by
NIYOGI BOOKS
Block D, Building No. 77,
Okhla Industrial Area, Phase-I,
New Delhi-110 020, INDIA
Tel: 91-11-26816301, 26818960
Email: niyogibooks@gmail.com
Website: www.niyogibooksindia.com

Editor: Sukanya Sur
Design: Shraboni Roy
Cover design: Duttatreya Ghosh

ISBN: 978-93-89136-03-6
Publication: 2019

Printed at: Niyogi Offset Pvt. Ltd., New Delhi, India

This novel is the story of the relationship between two very strong women of our times, who go through several rebirths in the course of their lifetimes. It carries certain traits of two of my previous novels, *Ami, Anupam* (*I, Anupam*), first published in Bengali in *Sharodiya Anandabazar* (1976), and my second novel, *Probashey Doiber Boshey* (*In a Foreign Land, by Chance*), first published in Bengali in *Sharodiya Krittibash* (1977). So, some of the faces of this novel are known. The rest will be introduced.

This novel was first published in Bengali as *Phoenix*. But in the translation, I decided to change the title to *The Parrot Green Saree*. I feel this title goes deeper into the soul of the text. *The Parrot Green Saree* is a story within a story. This tale of two generations will reveal how the new title is intrinsically related to the genesis of the story.

Nabaneeta Dev Sen

Bipasha

She was most reluctant to open her eyes, but there was no option. This daily pressure, this unavoidable circumstance of being forced, albeit unwillingly and distastefully, to perform one's duties had tortured Bipasha lifelong as had many other similar compulsions. Her mood was never good in the morning. She always felt tempted to switch off the alarm and go back to sleep. But she was very strict with herself about this from her college days. No matter how unwilling she was to get up, no matter how sleep clung heavily to every eyelash and drowned every pore of her body, she invariably woke up. Actually forced herself to get up. To be late in the morning meant the entire day's work getting delayed. Late for all appointments, the day not going as per schedule, therefore increasing the chance of failure, and that meant spoiling her work and leaving many chores incomplete. At long last, Bipasha had understood the essential lesson that your work is your life. Making love was equally important; it was impossible to imagine a life without love, but work preceded love. That's why laziness would never win in Bipasha's life. She was hardworking, enthusiastic, and ambitious. Whatever she had achieved was the result of her own efforts. In fact, her nature suited her name. She was independent, free-spirited, and unfettered. Life had taught her to live this way. Having lost her mother in childhood, she was the darling of her over-indulgent father on whose wish, although it was against her own, she lived abroad and alone for twenty years. Had she followed her own inclinations, she would have been languishing in some jail in West Bengal and not been a student of a prestigious college in Cambridge University. The circumstances changed when she was in her early twenties. A week spent in Czechoslovakia, observing the people of that country, their love for their nation and culture, witnessing their love for their mother tongue had generated in her a strange sense of security and self-confidence. Perhaps, Johan was responsible for this to a large extent. A sudden change had totally transformed a hitherto aimless Bipasha. Johan's harsh words rang in her ears. Why be afraid to return to one's native land? What could happen after all? May be a stint in the prison, that's all? Let that happen if it did, but Bipasha would not keep running away any longer. Her native land and her own language anchored her identity. Living in a foreign land made Bipasha think of herself as a crow with peacock feathers. She didn't think English had the right to be the language of her inner being. It could at best be the language of her education and thoughts. Her everlasting rights lay in the land that had been left behind, in its language and its culture. She was visiting the journal office with Samir the day Gourkishore Ghosh introduced her to Nirendranath Chakraborty saying, 'I know this girl since long. She was Anupam's student. She studied abroad and is professionally settled there. Her only fault is that she writes poems in English!' The statement had no intention to hurt or insult, but it had nearly changed Bipasha's life! It was as though on her return Bipasha was examining herself. She tried her best to return to her earlier days, but what could not happen did not happen. Can the past return? Nothing of what she had thought and wanted ever happened. Living again in her own land and in her own city seemed a painful experience that totally and entirely changed her from within. It was as if Bipasha sighed in relief to escape! Although words like 'escape' or 'running' did not appeal to her. The experience that did not empty a person was capable of enriching life. Bipasha was being enriched. Why should she remain confined when she possessed the key to explore the entire world? When the world was putatively expanding itself to show her its various pathways, why should she restrict herself within a small world and suffocate to death? Slowly, Bipasha was changing from the simple, idealistic, soft-hearted girl of her father's dreams to an individualistic, mature, internationally aware person who could live anywhere in the world, in whichever way she wished. To live as she wished did not mean being indisciplined. If one wanted life to be meaningful, some basic discipline was essential to succeed in any walk of life. Whether for a revolutionary lifestyle or for doing the simplest household chores, discipline was a must! Whoever you were, an artist or a businessman, it was tremendously necessary to possess innate clarity in understanding, and discipline in character.

Rohini was her own master. Bipasha used to think that Rohini did not have enough experience or maturity for that. Doing whatever one wished did not mean being completely enslaved by one's wishes. She could not make Rohini understand this simple fact. Rohini had to have it instantly whatever she wanted and whenever she wanted. If she didn't wish to wake up, she simply would not. If she didn't want to attend classes, she absolutely would not. If she didn't want to take the exam, no one could make her write it. If she wanted to see the Grand Canyon, she wanted to immediately start for it. With Rohini's exams nearing, Bipasha tried to stop her from going by refusing to give her money. But did that matter? No. With her little pocket money and loans from friends, she started off hitch-hiking with a friend. In her young days, Bipasha had hitch-hiked in Europe too; Rohini had heard those stories. It wasn't easy for two friends to hitch-hike. Often, the two of them would not fit into one car, so one had to wait for the next car. They had to fix a meeting place in the new city, being unsure when they would reach there. Usually, the meeting place would be a youth hostel. Those days, it was possible for students to travel like this in Europe; danger didn't lurk at every step. But Rohini did not understand that her mother's times had changed; hitch-hiking was not safe anymore, for either a man or a woman, and certainly not in America, neither for the person offering the lift nor for the person accepting it. Newspapers were full of reports about the dangers of hitch-hiking. Yet that girl went. She could surely do what her mother had done. In fact, she could do it even better! She had phoned her mother on reaching Arizona and also returned victorious and unharmed—but that was some time ago.

Rohini was arriving today. She just informed she was coming. Whether that would inconvenience her mother or whether her mother was free or not—the girl made no attempts to inquire. This irritated Bipasha. She felt offended. She was so highly respected in the academic community, Rohini knew it, but did not care. She had no respect for her mother.

❦

Bipasha was not a typical, emotional Indian mother. She felt insulted. She knew that for nothing and for nobody should one undervalue one's work. Nor could she. It was as though Rohini got some kind of pleasure in belittling her mother. She objected to everything concerning her mother. Everything displeased her—her lifestyle, her food habits, her choice of friends, her way of dressing—everything.

'Ma, what kind of dress is this? You look awful, please change.'

'Don't be silly! Look at it carefully, this is a designer dress by Calvin Klein!'

'May be, but it doesn't suit you. Wear something else. This is for tall women.'

'I like myself in this dress.'

'I am only trying to help you, Ma. This isn't suitable, trust me.'

'Why, what's wrong with it?'

'It makes you look old, Ma. It is meant for younger women.'

'Shut up, Rohini. Enough is enough!'

Bipasha was amused when she recalled this. Being an only child, Rohini's sibling rivalry seemed to be played out with her! She was irritated, but also felt sorry sometimes. Could there be any comparison between the two of them? But Rohini seemed to be competing with her all the time! Contesting Bipasha's fame, wealth, and influence was only Rohini's youth—and showing immaturity, even in that. There, too, was Bipasha's victory. She seemed to remain untouched by age. It could not be otherwise, she knew. She was always alert about that.

Rohini had always objected to Bipasha's young lovers. She could not tolerate any of them. But Bipasha was helpless. She needed men—and younger men stimulated her assertive sexuality. Perhaps, that was the main reason for Rohini's unspoken dissent.

'Ma, I feel very embarrassed. Why are you dating my friend? Aren't you ashamed to sleep with your daughter's friend?'

'Arre, what is there to feel ashamed about? This is really funny. Have I done anything with your Joey? Bobby isn't your boyfriend.

How is he your friend? What is this? He is much older to you. Bobby was my research student. In fact, you could ask why I date my students. So, he is no longer my student and he already has a job.'

'Chhi! Do you realize how old you are? You are an old woman, Ma, act your age! Leave the youngsters alone. If you can't do without men, then bring older men to your bed.'

Insults hurled by Rohini didn't bother Bipasha, didn't touch her at all. They amused her.

She laughed them away and said, 'Where will I get older men, tell me? Don't you see I am surrounded by the youth? Why don't you try to take your friends away from that circle? See if they go?'

Bipasha examined her nails and murmured to herself, 'I need a manicure, and also a pedicure, badly!'

Bipasha was reminded of Harry. Perhaps, Rohini was right about Harry. Or she was trying to respond to her mother's casual manner. In fact, she did not realize that her mother's heart was never really involved with those men. Bipasha had never shared her innermost thoughts with anyone. She couldn't think unless she was alone. She needed space. Men could stay as long as she needed them. In the realm of thoughts, Bipasha alone was the empress—no one could share that space. She could never make her daughter understand that in that innermost space, she reigned alone. Her daughter had tried to hurt her external pride by using that weak-minded Harry as a weapon.

'Ma, I won't stay here if Harry is here.'

'Why this, suddenly?'

'If I stay in this house, then Harry will not.'

'Don't talk like a fool. Why can't he?'

'Because I can't stand him, that horrible fellow. I really wonder at your taste—dirty beard, nasty, worthless artist, wears shabby clothes, spoils the walls, dirties the place by hanging his clothes all over....'

'But that's none of your business, Rohini dear.'

'It is. He looks at me in a horrible way. I hate him.'

'Say that, then. Why are you saying other things? Speak out.'

'He isn't good, Ma. He is your boyfriend. Why should he look at me in that way? Do my boyfriends stare at you like that?'

'Crazy girl! You are mistaken. You look so different, and you have such a special appearance that people can't help staring at you. Harry is an artist, he will certainly look. Don't misinterpret it.'

'How can you go around lecturing all over the place without understanding these things, Ma? You don't know people, you don't understand people. How can you write poetry?'

'Rohini!'

'He is bad, Ma, bad. Said he wanted to speak with me alone, wants to sketch me. Why should he say that? He is your boyfriend, let him sketch you.'

'He can always want to sketch you. You are very pretty. You look like a model, Ro!'

'Ma, you are acting funny, you know? Why are you so insensitive, Ma? About me?'

'Why are you being so rude to your mother?'

'Because she is insensitive about my problems. I tell you, Harry is bad material. Get rid of him fast. Don't blame me after this if anything happens. I have warned you.'

After this, Bipasha found Harry alone with Rohini doing a nude study. Harry was startled, but Rohini remained indifferent. Well, the danger passed with little harm. A vague fear had always clouded Bipasha's thoughts. It was no longer possible to continue her relationship with Harry. She had always feared that something like this would happen, but had ignored the thought since the warning came from Rohini.

Though Harry was a great lover, Bipasha threw him out. Rohini too left, not with Harry but alone. She headed straight to England to her father.

Rohini said before leaving, 'You don't care about my safety, you don't even listen when I warn you. I don't feel safe here.'

This was good, in a way. It wasn't really easy to keep an eye. It wasn't easy to live peacefully either. The daughter did not like any of her mother's lovers, although the latter certainly liked Rohini. Bipasha felt relieved to be free of this tension. Her daughter had lived with her for fourteen years; now let her father take care of her. The girl was already grown-up. It was late for getting admission that year. Rohini spent half the year enjoying a holiday with George and Eileen, Hugh and Don. She began her studies in England from the next session.

Rohini was arriving on a day when it wasn't possible for Bipasha to receive her at the airport. She had a very important meeting to attend. Very crucial. There was no way she could miss it. The annual executive meeting of the International Association of Postcolonial Studies was scheduled that day and Bipasha's name had been suggested as the president. It was very important for her to be present in the meeting today. The post was of great import. Standing against her was the eminent professor Okhardt. Professor Okhardt had steered postcolonial studies in Canada like Bhagirath. His fame was of longer duration, his age and academic weight were more. But Bipasha, being a woman and brown-skinned, had a heavy support group too. Additionally, her very popular book was already in the forefront as a flag of victory. Her book, *Under a Double Edged Sword: Postcolonialism and Women*, published by Melbourne Centre for Postcolonial Studies and based on her Mendelson Lectures delivered there, had already become widely accepted as a textbook everywhere. The book was on postcolonial theory and feminism. It argued that one could not equate Western feminism with that of Third World women whose life was much harder. They had to undergo more struggle, more pressures of consumerism and patriarchy, and they had to walk daily on paths strewed with thorns. This view had to be presented as a protest of a radically different kind than Western feminism. Whatever it may be, Bipasha knew the specificities of her thoughts and the theorization of her research. Not just the sharpness of logic, but also the fine structuring of her writing was responsible for the immense popularity of her book. Usually, books on postcolonial feminism were overburdened with complex theorization that undermined their clarity and interest. But Bipasha's book was very readable. Bipasha was a professor of English and Creative Writing and the subject of her particular interest was postcolonial literature. Other than this, she was a poet. Her poems in English had been published abroad for a long time. She already had four or five collections. But she never touched fiction. She had tried her hand at writing a novel, experimented with it in different ways for some time, and called it *The Parrot*

Green Saree, but hadn't completed it. Stubbornly, driven as though by an obsession, she had tried with great concentration to do her best; years passed but the writing did not proceed beyond the third chapter. She made several drafts, changed this and that, started afresh, cancelled everything to begin again....suddenly she realized and became acutely aware that she didn't have the patience to sustain a long narrative. Neither could she find new styles to adopt. In prose, writing articles was her forte, and in that, she was an expert of the first order. She was clearly a failure as a novelist. In life, what Bipasha hated the most was failure. She couldn't tolerate her own shameful failure. Those were the days of the typewriter, before the advent of the computer. She threw away the entire file of her aborted attempts at novel-writing in the waste basket to feed the incinerator, and wiped from her mind all traces of *The Parrot Green Saree*. Thus, Bipasha walked ahead in the path of life by continually erasing her past.

Now she was considering writing a memoir. This very year. She would begin it on her fifty-fifth birthday and move backwards. She can always return to the present in the next section. That was what she had decided; there was no chance of getting stuck, no threat of failure. For those who can write, the idea of a successful memoir was always in everybody's pocket. Bipasha knew that there was variety in her academic writing that successfully combined the heaviness of academic theorization with fine artistry of language use. She understood this well.

Her book on postcolonial feminism for students had won her many fans. Besides this, her foundational essays published in the *Journal of Postcolonial Studies* were requisite readings for researchers. She had a big group behind her in the International Association of Postcolonial Studies who wanted her as the president. Likewise, Okhardt, too, had a big support group who were determined to defeat Bipasha. Unless Bipasha was physically present in the meeting, it would be easy for the opposition to fight without any compunction. The current president Sri Lankan professor Vijay Bighnaraje had phoned her several times explaining the situation. David Marnoff of Princeton was standing for vice president's post. He had also spelt out clearly that it was imperative for Bipasha to be present at the meeting to win votes. This was also a requirement as per the election rules. Besides this, she had her own vote. Why should she waste that? President or vice president, no one is elected *in absentia*. Bipasha understood that the post of the president was important for enhancing international reputation, but it was also quite powerful. To win would mean becoming the head of the editorial board of the *Journal of Postcolonial Studies* for five years, as it was part of the responsibilities of the president of the association. This had tremendous possibilities. If she was elected, then she would be the first in two ways—the first woman president, and the first president from India. Considering all this, she had to attend the meeting.

But how would she explain all this to her immature and mindless daughter? Her daughter was coming home after so many years with her own child to stay with her mother! She had especially asked her mother to come to the airport to welcome them. This was both unexpected and slightly over the top. It was not possible to honour this request. But what was the point in getting irritated? The girl would simply not understand.

Gradually, Bipasha's impatience escalated. Could she imagine any reason for this? Why would Rohini cross the oceans to come here with her baby? What could be the reason for this? She never wanted anything from her mother. Was she then coming to teach a lesson to her uncaring mother? If nothing else, was this a way to defeat her mother? Did she plan to demonstrate how to be a good mother? Did she want to say that Rohini is giving her child the love, affection, and attention that Bipasha did not or could not give to the infant of her womb? This child wasn't even biologically Rohini's own. Suddenly, she thought of something which brought a trace of humour to her dissatisfaction—was Rohini trying to make her restless mother a stationary one? Would she find peace after introducing the third generation to make Bipasha a grandmother? Bipasha smiled. Rohini understood nothing about her.

Rohini's perennial complaint was that her mother was insensitive. Ma didn't understand her. Bipasha agreed that it wasn't possible for her to be a stereotypical mother. She never wished to be one at any cost. Rohini used to frequently remind her how she was becoming progressively insensitive towards her. How she never found her mother by her side when she needed her the most. Bipasha sometimes wondered if these were misunderstandings in Rohini's mind? Or did they truly show Bipasha's omissions?

'Ma, see, Diana isn't talking to me.'

'Okay, you too don't talk.'

'But she has my cycle.'

'Ask for it.'

'That means talking with her. But she doesn't answer.'

'Rohini, please don't drag me into these issues.'

'But I want to cycle now, Ma.'

'Fine, then take the cycle back from her.'

'But she isn't giving it back. She is cycling alone. How will I take it?'

'Learn to use some force, Rohini, or else others will take everything away from you.'

'Will you scold her a little, please, Ma?'

'Your mother won't solve your problems all through life. Remember you are alone in this world, so learn to solve your problems yourself.'

'But Ma....'

'Let me do my work, please!' Bipasha really had a lot of work. Rohini used to compare her with other mothers. She didn't understand that Bipasha's life was different. She had a goal to reach. Much work was yet to be done. How could she leave everything and sit down with her daughter in her lap? Besides, she wanted her daughter to learn the necessary lessons of life. Life had taught her that no one will do anything for you if you can't grab it yourself. Today, Rohini was so independent that she could ignore everything and take the responsibility of an infant. Didn't Bipasha have any role to play in this?

Rohini had always believed that her mother understood nothing. But Bipasha felt no guilt over that. She knew that when everyone left, when everything was gone, the one thing that would keep her alive and be her haven was the inner world of her mind. The refuge of her intellect. Her work. Her daughter wouldn't appreciate this. The girl could never stick to any work for long; she had to do whatever her whimsy dictated. She had kept herself away, as though deliberately, from the academic world. Bipasha had nothing to say about this. She thought it was fortunate that the girl had gone away to her father after falling out with her mother over the issue with Harry. She had a lifelong squabble with her mother. Daily confrontations, misunderstandings, and insult.

'Dave, Dave, you can't do this to me! No, you can't.'

'Ma, Ma! Do you know, Dave went for a movie with Sara! Ma, he can't do this to me.'

'Okay, leave him. There are many boys in the world. Dave is not the only one.'

'Oh, Ma, he is my boyfriend. Why did he—with Sara … ?'

'That happens sometimes. It's nothing, don't take it seriously. Why don't you too go for a movie with John, Tom, or somebody? Tit for tat!'

'Ma, you don't understand. We are in love!'

'Look, my baby, you may be in love, but obviously Dave is not. You must take this as a hint for you. It's a clear hint. And, honey, you had better look for someone else now.'

'Ma, I said we are in love. You don't seem to realize. Can't you understand this?'

'I do, Ro dear. I perfectly understand. It's you who doesn't, baby. You don't understand that Dave is thinking differently….'

'Why? Why should he think differently?'

'He has changed his mind. These things happen. And it will happen many times. Darling, you are only fourteen. It's not yet the age to fall in love, honey. It's fun time. Don't mope around, it's nothing serious….'

'Ma, how could you talk like this? Love is nothing serious?.... You could say this?'

'I am only trying to protect you, Ro. You better protect yourself.'

'Ma, have fun yourself. You needn't bother about me. Okay? It was my mistake to have come to you. With three broken marriages behind you, and an endless string of stupid lovers, you know nothing about love, Ma! How can you advise me?'

This perhaps was true. May be, Bipasha really did not know what love was? Once she had believed that she knew. But after that rainy evening with Samir at Bagha Jatin, she forced herself to 'unlearn' what she knew love to be. She could not recollect at the moment the correct Bengali word for 'unlearn'. The value of what that one evening had snatched away from Bipasha was a lot, but it had given her much more. She knew the value of what she had received—the Bipasha Anderson of today.

Bipasha could not grasp why Rohini was inflicting this torture on her. To punish her for some fault? She knew Bipasha couldn't tolerate children—she had explained this frankly to her. It had been maddening to mind her own child. She had never wanted to be a mother. When she realized that the unwanted child had entered her womb, it was too late for abortion. Since it had come, she let it remain. What option was there? But that didn't mean that Bipasha was ready to sign a bond of slavery with the child. She couldn't stay alive if she wasn't free. Every relationship in her life had to be open-ended. No way could it be under lock and key, otherwise she would suffocate and the relationship would wither. She married three times, attempting to build a home. This had not been possible. The husbands weren't to blame. They were all simple social beings; they weren't bad.

Each time, it was her fault that all the three marriages came to an end. She was the misfit. That was when she realized that she needed love; without love she wouldn't know herself. She needed to see herself through the eyes of her lovers. That gaze was required to maintain her youthful confidence. She could see her academic reflection in her papers, seminars, and response of her students in class. There was no dearth of confidence in herself as an intellectual; she felt no inadequacy in that. But the other Bipasha, the one who wrote poems, knew that without intense love she wouldn't be able to write poetry. The lovers' gaze maintained her youth and kept her poetry alive. But any kind of bondage, even in that, would be fatal. Relationships were needed, passionate relationships, but no shackles. She could sustain only those relationships that remained unfettered. George was that kind of a friend. He happened to be the father of her unwanted child after they became involved in an unintended relationship. The first husband of her life, George still remains her friend. They now knew each other completely like siblings. There were no unfamiliar dark corners, no fear of taking a false step. They expected nothing from each other except good wishes.

One bond remained between them however—Rohini.

Whether she wanted or not, the mischance of becoming a mother had happened in her life. No matter how much she tried, Bipasha could not shrug away, like a drop of water from the feathers, the burden of motherhood from her life.

Motherhood meant bondage.

Bipasha never wanted bondage.

Rohini will arrive soon. With her child. Her plane will land after breakfast. Bipasha won't go to the airport. She had asked Disha to bring Rohini home. Not just Rohini, but the two of them. Mother and daughter. Good that Chris was not in the city that day. Rohini would have become resentful on seeing him and might have started misbehaving with them both. She behaved fine when she was in a good mood. But when she wasn't? Then there was no control over what she did or said. But that didn't mean Bipasha would live her life according to others' convenience. Her wishes didn't matter in Rohini's life, but Rohini wanted Bipasha's life to run as per her wishes. Since that wasn't allowed to happen, the distance between mother and daughter had increased day by day. But Bipasha considered this a healthy prospect. Rohini was still young, so she didn't appreciate this as the best way to sustain their individual freedom. If Bipasha had to spend her life according to Rohini's wishes, then Rohini herself would have been trapped in a larger web of responsibilities. And that would not have been a happy situation. This was much better—the two of them at two opposite coasts of the Atlantic, both independent, both free—although mothers were always less free from day one, whether they wanted it or not. No matter how much she denied this, as she was ageing, she had begun to feel a certain degree of helplessness from within. The thought of this always made her uncomfortable

She had to get up now. Whether the alarm sounded or not, she was now wide awake and could sleep no longer.

After extending her arm to switch off the phone alarm, Bipasha realized that she was actually using these random and irresolvable thoughts to laze longer in bed. Nothing more. Really, human mind knew various ways of deception. We are really matchless in deceiving ourselves.

Cautiously, Minto approached her feet and pushed gently. This was his way of greeting her every morning. A reminder that it was time for his biscuits and walk. There was no place for deception in Minto and his kind.

❦

Hridaypure joteelotar cholitechhilo khela—Complex games were being played in the realm of the heart.

No, it was really time to get up. Minto should not be kept waiting for his morning chores. She stepped out of bed and pulled the silk cord to open the heavy window curtains apart. Rather like the magical '*khul ja sim sim*' charm, the glistening gems of light irradiated the dark room. Great, the day was lovely! Now Minto had to be let out in the garden. She opened the door and picked up her spectacles from the bedside table, then poured herself a glass of cold water to drink. She suddenly recalled that the glass was one from the set of crystal glasses received as gift in Czechoslovakia. Bechka's gift. Yohan, Mirko, Evichko, Evichka. Bratislava seemed a distant dream—the Budmerice Palace surrounded by orchards and forests, roaming about the expanse with a flock of turkeys strutting around, and sometimes spotting the plumage of the Indian peacock! The deeper parts of the forest still retained the winter frost on the ground. There was no other sign of winter. On a small mound of snow, Yohan had planted a leafy branch and joked, 'We have now conquered this mountain peak and here we plant our flag of victory!' Then, those two days and two nights spent at Nitra. The present Bipasha was a different person. But those two days spent in that small hillside town of Nitra had changed all calculations of Bipasha's life. Putting the glass of water down, Bipasha wore her specs and looked at herself in the mirror. Good morning, Bipasha! The full-length mirror stood in front. Feng Shui advises that one mustn't sleep with a mirror in front. Bipasha didn't believe all that. Where else would such a big mirror fit? She needed light, walls, and privacy. Only that wall had no bookshelves. There was also a window beside it. Her dressing items were all in the bathroom. There were big, half-size mirrors there; it also had a dressing table. This long mirror was meant for sarees. It showed a full-length reflection, and there was a light fitted to the mirror too. She gazed at the mirror and examined her reflection carefully. Her heart-shaped face was surrounded by tousled, curly black hair with a reddish tint, and the eyes under the black brows were sharp with intelligence, but the pale, lipstick-free lips were the opposite—they appeared soft, sad, and sensitive, like coffee with extra milk. She turned this way and that, raised and lowered her head, and stared closely at herself. She wasn't tall, but had an enviable figure, hard to miss. Slim, light, and petite. Who could guess that she was a highly placed professional and a mother of a grown-up girl? She knew that those who did not know her would be tempted to refer to her as 'that girl'. She gymed and practised yoga regularly, and maintained a healthy diet. On every holiday, she went for swimming and aerobics. She took good care of her body and health and tried to maintain a well-balanced lifestyle, though she was well aware that her invisible, inner life was not so. She understood that for successful mental activity, keeping the body healthy was essential. Be it a woman or a man, health and beauty were equally useful. Neither was she casual in her dressing. She was never the typical absent-minded professor. She was not the kind to step out wearing one shoe in one foot and another from a different pair. Whatever she wore at home, at work, at parties—all were meticulously selected. She was always well made-up and wore matching jewellery, not excessive but unusual in style. Whatever she purchased, she did so with conscious attention—for foreign dresses, she would be careful about the brands, style, and fashion. She had no problem in spending money and regarded clothes as an expression of one's identity. Right clothes and style conveyed one's taste, wisdom, and power. The mirror reflection showed her in her nightwear. This particular pyjama-suit in printed cotton with vegetable dyes was a favourite of hers. Her sister bought it from a handloom exhibition somewhere. The set came with a matching housecoat. Disha had good taste. Slipping her feet into the bedroom slippers, she recalled that this footwear was also gifted by Disha. They were very nice, made of cane and leather. She found Disha very compatible, though she wasn't like her. Once a district magistrate, she was now an IAS officer and posted in Delhi. Her husband was also in Delhi. While brushing her teeth, Bipasha thought that government officer couples seldom got their posting together. Usually, the husband and wife were posted at different places, and working mothers often found it difficult to bring up a child and had to opt for sending the kid to a boarding school. But Disha and her husband enjoyed the rare opportunity of being posted in Delhi together. However, they had no children and yearned for one. Those who desire children are often denied the chance, while others get unwanted children. She knew this from her own experience. Women were not all born bearing ready-made mothers in their heart. Much of it came from habit. For instance, she had had no preparation to welcome a child. It had tied up her life in knots. Bipasha had no faith in God or fate. She had been trained from her early youth in atheism, as a Naxal. Whom could she blame?

The word 'Naxal' immediately brought to mind two names—Anupam Roy and Samir. Bipasha felt a bitter taste in her mouth.

It was her habit to examine her face in the magnifying mirror in the bathroom for telltale signs of age. She looked carefully today too. Were their two fine lines lurking at the corner of her eyes? Crow's feet? No, lines of age were not yet manifest on her face. Not for Disha either. To her, Disha's complexion still appeared clear like a child's. But how did she appear in others' eyes?

Rohini had admonished her ten years ago, 'Ma, act your age.' Bipasha wondered what was meant by ageing? Her menopause had come about four years ago. Her current lover wasn't a sprightly youth either. But age? Bipasha became thoughtful.... But she was getting late, she must go for her bath.

She wore her shower cap and carried the shower gel as she stood under the shower. The hexagonal shower cubicle was a new addition in the bathroom. Beside it, she had installed a matching brass-bordered, semi-circular jacuzzi bath. For days that were less busy. She was especially fond of the soft touch and fragrance of the peach-blossom shower gel. She had arranged a regular supply from a particular spa in the countryside. The orange aloe vera face wash gel and the after-bath rose-petal body lotion were also sourced from the same place. Physical care didn't mean just exercise. Shouldn't the skin be nurtured? How else would there be a glow? Jethima was very attentive about these matters. She used to make various concoctions for skin care like butter with skimmed milk, pounded lentils, sesame oil, raw turmeric paste, dried orange peel paste, and so on to be applied forcibly on the two sisters. That felt so bad then. Dada or Chorda didn't have to bear such torture. Bipasha and Bidisha were two cousins in a joint family.

Bipasha had never wanted to be a mother; she didn't like children. Whether a boy or a girl, to her all children were boring and selfish. Her thoughts hadn't changed. Children were self-centred and totally physical, fully body-centric. They could use others so well to suit their own purpose, as though the entire world was their slave. They claimed to be weak, inarticulate, and dependent. Bipasha hadn't noticed it earlier, but her stay abroad showed the pitiful condition of women all around her. Intensely distasteful to her was the sight of pram-pushing mothers enslaved in the trap of their motherly love, the custom-made helpless existence. No, that kind of entangled life was not acceptable to Bipasha. She wanted to be liberated, solitary. Free spirit. She would use her creativity for her own self. For her poetry. She would use it to make her academic identity strong and distinguished. Was a human being's creativity limited to the testicles and the womb? Creativity's rightful place was in the intellect. Union was wholesome joy. She wasn't disinterested in physical pleasure. The centuries-old closed door had opened for her. Right after that rainy day. But she was a practical person and never forgot to be careful. Always, the fear of becoming pregnant had preceded physical pleasure.

This was her state of mind when she learnt from the doctor that she was carrying a child and it was more than thirteen weeks old. Nowhere in England would she be allowed to abort at this stage. For some time past her body had been sending different kinds of signals, the count of days had become confused. She hadn't grasped this fact at all. But George was very happy. He immediately proposed marriage and began to take extra care of her. Their marriage happened and the child was born without any hassle. There were no physical complications. The entire complication was in Bipasha's mind.

Mainly, it was George who looked after the baby and did so very happily. He would bring the baby to Bipasha from time to time so she could feed her. Other than that, George didn't let her feel any burden. George's job allowed him to work from home. Bipasha was then engrossed in writing her thesis and

George ensured in different ways that she got maximum time with her books. Bipasha's poetry, Bipasha's PhD—George deeply respected every aspect of her work. He owned his family business, had enough helpers in office, was sufficiently wealthy, but hadn't got the chance to pursue higher education. He didn't have the stamp of the university. The crack in Bipasha's relationship with George began from that shadowed spot. Although he was totally successful in every way in his own profession, emotionally George felt incomplete and unaccomplished because he hadn't been able to go for higher studies. Bipasha could not bear the proximity of an unsuccessful man for long. She had been forced to marry George because of Rohini; she did not hesitate now to break the marriage and free herself. George did not stop her, nor did he show any bitterness. He only wanted Bipasha to do whatever she wanted for her career. She had his consent. Meanwhile, George had realized that even if Bipasha had affection for him, she did not respect him.

Rohini was then three years old. There was no problem in getting custody of a child till eight years. But the mother didn't want the child's responsibility. Her father earned much more, so she let him take care of her. The mother had a lecturer's job in America along with postdoctoral fellowship, but without a tenure track. George happily agreed to be the guardian. But the objection came from the girl. She didn't want to leave her mother. She cried hugely and insisted that she wanted to stay with her mother. Bipasha's father was delighted with his granddaughter. He came to England on the slightest excuse to see her. He added to the pressure that she could not leave behind such a small child. Because Bipasha had lost her mother very early, she did not realize how important it was for the child to live with her mother. Bipasha did not oppose her father. He never imposed his views on Bipasha; whenever he suggested something, it had been for her good. Very unwillingly, Bipasha carried her encumbrance to America and that increased her grudge towards her daughter. Her new job outside and childcare at home—Bipasha was most unwilling to bear the twin burden. She grew more impatient with the child's various demands on her time. Being conscious of the situation and aware that his daughter would face difficulty, George began to send generous sums to Bipasha for childcare. An Indian lady was employed to babysit. Mrs Nalini Patel came to take care of the child and cook small items. Rohini had been away from her mother for many years, but Mrs Patel still came once in seven days and cooked for the week. Bipasha was not interested in housekeeping and regarded it as a waste of time. When she earned enough, she employed another person to take care of the house. Mrs Smith came once a week and stayed the whole day. Bipasha's household ran perfectly. Her lovers were also very useful and helped her in many little ways. They respected her too. Her lovers were always younger to her, not only lesser in age but in other ways also. They gazed at her in admiration with fanlike attentiveness. That was their USP. Bipasha thoroughly enjoyed that. And that was exactly what young Rohini could not tolerate.

They hadn't met for a long time. Rohini e-mailed her mother from time to time, but she rarely phoned. On the other hand, her contact with George was fairly regular. George called regularly to ask about her. Rohini hadn't returned since she left home after their quarrel when she was fourteen years old. Bipasha, too, had not made any efforts to bring her back. She knew the girl had gone to George where she would be happier; in fact, both would be in good cheer. Rohini had been wilful here, but she won't be so in her father's house. Certain rules had to be followed there. George's wife Eileen was a busy housewife, looking after her husband and children. She was a teacher in a government nursery school close by. She was a nice person and had time on her hand. They had no daughter, but two small boys. Rohini liked living in Eileen's household. No, her own mother had no interest in family or household, though she had all that one would need besides helpers at hand. There was no problem. Her mother did nothing by herself. Rohini was upset. Why didn't she cook daily like other mothers? What was the need for Mrs Patel? She didn't like her mother's young lovers; they claimed whatever free time her mother could spare. How much time did her mother spend with her? Why should they come? Why should they stay with her mother? Bipasha was busy with her travels, meetings, readings, and lectures—Rohini disliked all this intensely. Her mother was always busy with her work, or with her lovers. Where was the time to spare for Rohini? She observed from childhood that her mother became irritated if Rohini went close to her. Work, work, and work all the time. When there were readings in the city, her mother took her along to show how much she was respected. After she grew up, neither did her mother call her, nor did she want to go.

Rohini had never accepted the matter of her mother's lovers. She had shown her disapproval in the case of the men her mother married, but she had not created problems. They were of suitable age, and sometimes an affectionate relationship had developed with her, as for example with Virendra. She had even learnt Hindi from him. Then there was Larry. Although he was such a well-known linguist, Larry showed no interest in his work. But he could really entertain youngsters. Rohini liked him. But, for Bipasha, neither was acceptable as lifelong partners. So the relationships broke both times. The random lovers was another matter. They were short-lived contacts, they came and went, and they couldn't even put a tether to the threshold of life. Rohini refused to accept them. This led to strong disagreements and dissent with her mother. Bipasha understood this, but she couldn't help it. She needed young lovers. How would she maintain her vibrant youth if hormones weren't properly activated? The girl would never understand this, and so her unreasonable opposition would never end and the contradiction between them would never cease. If the mother became upset to see her daughter, grew overly anxious or irritated, then what could be done? This was a mechanical nervous reaction. Bipasha had hoped that this illogical melancholy would end someday. But actually, instead of the melancholy, irritation, and anxiety for the young daughter ending, the worrisome mental condition escalated. The age gap between the daughter and the mother's lovers was decreasing.

Bipasha had hoped that as Rohini grew older, mother and daughter would gradually get to know each other better and accept each other in the usual manner of the modern adult world. There would be an end to their misunderstandings. Once she finished college. But there was no time for logical explanations. Rohini left home in a rage much before that, throwing her passport, credit card provided by her father, and a few clothes in her rucksack. She continued her studies in England and did not return to her mother. She got her news regularly from George; but she felt no emotional response to her daughter's absence. It wasn't as though they didn't meet at all; they had, here and there, several times through the years. That small girl was now a grown-up and attractive young woman. She looked very Indian with her waist-long black hair, black eyes, and heart-shaped face. Rohini liked to stress on the Indian touch in her dressing style also. There was a clear resemblance with Bipasha, but she had also inherited her father's skin colour and figure. Rohini was quite tall. Yes, there may have been efforts from both sides, but the bridge was not built.

Bipasha wondered if she could finish some shopping before the girl's abrupt arrival. She couldn't do it the last Saturday. Mrs Elizabeth Smith came every Friday and stayed the whole day, cleaning the house, washing the vessels, changing bed linen, washing, drying, and ironing clothes. She arranged the potted plants, hosed the garden and watered the plants, and switched on the sprinkler in the lawn. Then she cleaned and dusted the carpet, and vacuumed the bookshelves. Elizabeth had become old and was slightly hard of hearing. Bipasha planned to get her tested for a hearing aid. She was a black woman; they hadn't managed yet to stop early pregnancies in their community. Her young daughter was already a grandmother. But the family had no male member. This, too, was typical. Most black families in the city were mainly matriarchal. A male member meant problems, with their many demands to sustain their substance abuse. And bear their battering besides that. It was better to do without a father. Elizabeth had tremendous energy, physically and mentally, and also a deep affection for Bipasha's household. The house shone in its cleanliness. She regularly polished the silverware and lamps. She also ensured a ready supply of small items like milk, coffee, etc. She checked the larder and left Bipasha a list of what needed to be replenished. Elizabeth was a huge asset in Bipasha's busy professional life.

Mrs Nalini Patel also continued. Her husband now had his own shop managed by his daughter and son-in-law. The corner store sold everything from newspapers, chocolates, cigarettes, milk, soft drinks like coke, bread, eggs, fruit, and shaving kits even over the counter medicines like aspirin, Tylenol, and so on. Mrs Patel came once a week, cooked for four days, and put it in the fridge. From steaks, biriyani, Hungarian goulash to sambar-masala dosa—from Indian to continental, she had learned all kinds of cuisines. She had come as a young bride and her husband used to work in a small store. She used to be Rohini's babysitter. The relationship had endured for two decades. On the remaining days, Bipasha either got food ordered from outside or cooked something light herself. But not daily cooking. She liked trying new recipes sometimes. Chris, too, was very enthusiastic about cooking. He often said that he could manage alone, that there was no need for Mrs Patel. Let him say that; he was after all a man saying that in a spurt of overenthusiasm. He could easily say tomorrow that he had no time, that he can't do all that. Bipasha was wise; she didn't relinquish her daily dependence on Mrs Patel. She knew well that because of these women, the two pillars of her household, she could lead such a free life. She could make space for romance in her life whenever she wished. She enjoyed that sense of peace. Being a woman, busy with several serious responsibilities, that kind of peace was difficult to obtain, especially in this country where it wasn't easy to get help.

Having finished her bath, she wore her housecoat and went to the kitchen to brew coffee in the coffee maker. She took from the fridge strawberry, yogurt, apple juice, and eggs. And the box of muesli from the shelf. This was a very nutritious and appetizing breakfast made with different kinds of seeds, dried fruit, nuts, and almonds. Once, it used to be made only in Switzerland; one had to buy this from health food stores in England and America. It was now available everywhere. Bipasha was very fond of muesli, but Chris didn't like it. He preferred toast and eggs. Placed in a large wooden bowl on the dining table were apples, bananas, and oranges. Bipasha kept cutlery, plates, and coffee mugs ready not in the dining room but on the kitchen table, covered with a checked tablecloth. The table covered with the white-and-cream-checked tablecloth had, as a centrepiece, a small, red money plant spreading its thin white roots in the water in a round, clear glass vase. This morning Chris was away from the city. Had he been home, he would have had their breakfast ready. This was his department. Sometimes, if she had worked late at night, he lovingly brought her breakfast in bed, arranged on a tray. Chris enjoyed doing these things. He wasn't here this morning. She set the table for herself, sipped from the glass of apple juice, and wondered what to eat—there was indeed a wide choice. Two strawberries in muesli? Or, an omelette, without the egg yolks, along with strawberries? The coffee was gurgling to announce it was ready. Ah, the wonderful aroma of freshly ground coffee filled the kitchen. Bipasha had always been a devotee of coffee. Samir used to laugh about this. The bitter and manly taste of large roasted coffee beans was very dear to her. Bipasha decided, as she poured coffee into the tall, decorated Tibetan mug brought from China, that she would opt for muesli this morning since Chris was away.

Jibon giyechhe choley kurri kurri bochhor paar ... Life has gone on for two-score years ...

These days Bipasha recalled her childhood days frequently. Disha and her husband had come to Harvard on special study leave permitted to IAS officers. The two sisters met regularly. Many old stories came up. Many issues from their young days that had never been mentioned earlier were also discussed. Age. Maturity. Earlier they didn't have that much understanding about either. Bidisha was called 'Disha' at home and Bipasha was 'Tuku'. Disha had remained a younger sister to her didibhai for a long time. Even after clearing the IAS exam. Only after she took charge as district magistrate was she accepted by her didi as having attained maturity. Life had taught Bipasha many lessons; the main lesson was to respect success. It goes without saying that the opposite lesson she had taught herself was to despise failure. There was no place in her life for unsuccessful individuals. Time was short, it had to be spent with care. She understood successful people. That had some simple, countable basic rules. But being unsuccessful could have two hundred twenty-two reasons. She wasn't Mother Teresa; she had no sympathy for non-success. It was worthless making effort and wasting time to understand why one was unsuccessful. No, she wouldn't do that. In fact, the actual reason for her marriages to fail was her impatience and scorn for failure. She couldn't stay with Virendra because he had no ambition himself and tried to interfere in hers. That she understood. But what she didn't understand was why she fell in love repeatedly with unsuccessful men? Except for George. How did that go haywire? That was the first time since she left her native country that she was returning very upset. She met George on the plane. After that, a long time passed in a sort of daze … until Rohini announced her presence. On George's insistence and his help, her doctoral work progressed and she got her degree in three years. She had much to be grateful for to George. George was generous, warm, and honest. Yet, she couldn't ultimately stay with him. George was very boring. Both had tried to make their relationship work, but though he was a good friend, there was a big difference between George's personality and hers. Did that make Rohini's life chaotic? Rohini had been in her care in the beginning, then as a teenager she went away to her father. George was a much better guardian than her. He did not have much outside interests. Neither did he have overarching ambition. He was content to remain where he had already arrived, with no further demands from life. And, Rohini, to him, was like a special prize. Bipasha had done this job well; she hadn't asked Rohini to return. She did not accept the excuse offered by the doctor for falling in love with unsuccessful people. There was no lack of successful men in her life. In her professional career, she interacted with the most successful people in the world. They constituted her circle. Successful men did fall for her; people suitable for her love were very much there. But her relationships remained stuck at mere flirtation, they didn't develop into love. The brake would come from her inner being. She couldn't surrender herself completely.

Chris was not a toy boy like her earlier lovers. This relationship had lasted a few years. Something like friendship had grown with him. A man's company was needed to keep her mind and body vibrant. She saw no use for falling in love for the sake of love. Making love is something, and falling in love is something else. Bipasha Anderson had no time to spare for emotions. She needed a man's warm, admiring companionship. No need for love. The earlier relationships were light-hearted, simple, and short-lived. She got bored very quickly. Her relationship with Chris was becoming slightly different.

Disha and her husband were due to visit today. They had planned to go to the Niagara Falls this weekend. Will Rohini be here then? She said nothing about how long she will stay. Rohini was totally opposite of her mother. She had no attraction for knowledge; her father was closest to her. Bipasha had noticed that Rohini valued lack of success more. And she tried her best to even shape herself as an unsuccessful person. Was that to hurt her? Rohini knew Disha and Anubhav well; she had stayed with them in Delhi. Still, as much as she knew her, Rohini was a moody girl; no one could say how she would behave with others. Disha and Anu did not fall in the category of unsuccessful people; in fact, they were just the opposite. They would surely understand, no matter what her mood was like. They wouldn't mind.

Her sister's husband hailed from Odisha. Anubhav Mohapatra, a fine person, was now a joint secretary. Disha was younger to Bipasha by five years; she grew up after the Naxal wave had passed. Their generation didn't have to suffer any disturbance in their education. She was cool-headed, practical, and intelligent from her childhood. Bipasha had to bear much to safeguard herself, after the upheaval, disturbance, and stormy squall had blown over.

When the police found the kitbag in Professor Anupam Roy's house and visited Gautamda's father's tutorial home, Bipasha's father flew to Mumbai with his daughter that very night. If Samir and others were caught, the police would torture them to get the names of others. Her father got their visa done and left immediately for England. He didn't allow her to waste time, but got her admitted in a night college in London. Disha was still in school, studying in a higher class. While she was growing up, her didibhai was engrossed in political intrigue. When she was at home, she played the role of dumb, deaf, and mute. No friendship developed between adolescent Disha and her didi. In fact, due to the revolutionary demands of secrecy, Bipasha had become very alone at home. She hardly spoke, nor did she spend much time there. Her relationship with her father had reached the worst point. But, from the time of making arrangements for her escape from Kolkata, her father took over all responsibility for her future. They had no monetary difficulty. Her father stayed in England and made arrangements for Bipasha's admission into Newnham College of Cambridge University to study English from the next session. He introduced her to his schoolmate Babukrishan's sister Sita Chari. Sita had been a brilliant student and was then a professor of English at Cambridge. Her father entrusted Bipasha to her after explaining everything. Bipasha was also a good student from Presidency, but she was no longer concentrating on her studies. Accepting the chairman of China as their own chairman, a group of sharp, bright, visionary boys and girls were sacrificing their present and future to fight for the deprived and the oppressed people of their own country. She was one of them. Chorusing the victory of Mao Zedong, they had undertaken the task to save the good and annihilate the evil to re-establish dharma in society! They had not reflected upon whether the path of destruction they had chosen was right or wrong. They had full faith in their ideals and leadership. Whatever cruelty happened was all in the service of the greater good, for the benefit of their impoverished country. Then things became anarchic. Accused of inciting insurrection and of provoking murder and mayhem, those whom the police wanted, the older guerilla leaders, kept shifting their hideouts, took shelter behind the younger ones, and lived in their shadow and their pledge of life and death. Those who got arrested were the restless groups of younger people. But the honourable intellectuals who were visible in the public eye as the supporters of the revolution, who wrote to buttress their political philosophy and boost their morale, and who had willingly become their guide and guardian when they, too, became entangled in police action and legal issues, thought it safer to retreat than getting involved with the police. To protect their self-interest in times of crisis, even breaking trust as proof of their extreme cowardice, they distanced themselves without the least hesitation. They ran away not just mentally or professionally, but removed themselves physically out of West Bengal, if not out of India on some pretext. Some went to Delhi, some to America, some to England. And some took off from their work too, citing ill health. Defeated and betrayed by the elders, the groups of young people lost faith in themselves, and became alone, adrift, and vulnerable. The result of this was disastrous. They faced either premature death at the hands of the police, or long and bitter imprisonment. The revolution at the cost of numerous lives did not appear successful. But the failed cause congealed in the minds of the so-called revolutionaries and became knotty. These festered as problems and bitterness in life. Quite a few of these youngsters who had managed to evade the police and escape with the help of their families, lived their lives but as radically changed individuals. They, too, could not entirely escape the mental knots and never found peace from the haunting sense of having betrayed their companions.

Bipasha found a place for herself at Cambridge. The university life helped her to remake herself and give her a new sense of life.

Not just with studies, it was as though her acquaintance with the world began anew. Some afternoons she would cycle with her friends to Grantchester for lunch; some days she went to watch a play at London. With Sita's help, she joined a group of young student poets who had formed a literary group called Poets' Circle. A famous poet, Sita's friend, was associated with them as a mentor. He accepted Bipasha eagerly. She used to write poetry secretly at home, but didn't show anybody since it was in English. After losing her mother in childhood, her schooling in a hill-station boarding school had made her more confident in English than in her mother tongue. She used to write to Samir in English. Samir was upset with her for this; he said that this distanced her from people and prompted alienation. She should speak in the language spoken by others, even write in it. Mistakes didn't matter; after all, that was her mother tongue, whatever she wrote was right. But no matter what was said, Bipasha felt shy to write in Bangla. Her Bangla was very poor and could even become laughable at times. There were such good poets around her. She could read the language fluently, of course; their house was full of Bangla books belonging to her mother. While at college, in Kolkata, she used to learn Bangla songs at Dakshini; she had no trouble reading *Gitabitan*. Samir used to gift her Bangla books and she liked reading Bangla poetry. Her problem was in writing it. Samir used to tease her, calling English 'handful of rice thrown as alms by the colonizers', so she never showed her English poems to anyone. Hence, what she wrote, sense or nonsense, got no feedback. There was no way to know that without readers. Now, in England, she renewed writing poems freely in English, sitting in a group of fellow poets. Reading poems in Poets' Circle was followed by a discussion of one another's poems; good and bad both were discussed and analysed. This helped her the most. And English? That was the language of expression of every individual in this country. Everyone in the group wrote in that language. It wasn't as though all were from Britain. There was a boy from Africa, a boy from Turkey, and a girl from Pakistan. Like Bipasha, they were more confident in English; it seemed easier to express their thoughts and feelings in that language. How easy it was to express thoughts of the postcolonial mind in the calm waters of the victors' language! She was fortunate to get a familiar person like Sita as her tutor. She received her affectionate encouragement in every way. After obtaining good grades and a degree in English from Cambridge, Bipasha did not continue her studies after graduation. She concentrated on writing and was working in a reasonably known British publication house. Meanwhile, she considered whether to start her PhD under Sita. It was possible to do a PhD in Cambridge after a tripos. A master's degree automatically followed after two years of attaining tripos. No separate examination was required. One could submit requisite money and the form, wear the gown, and collect the degree during convocation. Very few people took it, however. Within a short time, Bipasha Choudhury had become well known among the young poets of England as an Indian poet in English. At that time, she had acquired many friends who were artists, who did not believe in mundane living, but in experimentation in life. Such friends were the president of London's Race Relations Board, the elderly American Jimmy Watchman, and his even older wife, Kelly. Every weekend they held mesmerizing night-long meetings in the basement of their three-storied home in Finchley. Their basement was a very spacious hall without walls. Besides little food items, there would be on offer a variety of hallucinogens. In fact, to Bipasha it seemed like an illegal den of drugs. There was innocuous hash, grass, and marijuana, along with other types of banned supply like brown sugar, coke, LSD tablets—what wasn't there? And there was the communion of old abusers with new addicts. Vocalists, instrumentalists, writers, painters, journalists, publishers, photographers—all kinds of artistes of the society met there—white, black, yellow, brown—all would come. They would sit, lounge, or lie on mats or carpets spread on the floor and engage in their unsocial socialization. In the haze of drugs, poems were read, and songs and music were played, along with passionate and public lovemaking until drowsiness overtook all. If one could emerge like a saint from that trap and network correctly, it was possible to advance in the world of art and literature. Bipasha had tried to get into that group for a while. She went a few times on Jimmy's and Kelly's invitation and understood that if she could make the correct connections, there was a good chance of advancing her career. But she couldn't continue. Her taste stopped her. Her inner being objected. She was still the earlier Bipasha who didn't think of future benefit. She ran away from there, saying, 'To hell with art!' Every pore and every nerve of her body used to rebel if she went there. What was this anarchy in the name of art? She couldn't go there after the first couple of times. Much better was the hippy commune at Betty's house in Muswell Hill. About ten or twelve boys and girls occupied the entire third floor of an old house and lived in a commune, much like a joint family. One contributed to a common fund as per one's earning. The person earning more would contribute more; if someone didn't earn, one needn't pay at all. It had many kinds of people. There were two or three children also. An infant grew up in the midst of others in the commune. A mother had left her baby and ran away, while the father wrote songs, played guitar, and worked in someone's garden. The child was everybody's responsibility. Another's child was going to school; the mother was still a student and the grandmother was taking care of the child. She, too, was a young person, a reporter in a local paper, and a poet. Someone was attending the veterinary college and worked as a model; another drew pictures and drove a truck. But there was also quiet drug-sharing. At night, in a dark room, under psychedelic lights, someone would play guitar, some would sing, while some recited poems. They would sit in a circle and pass marijuana and grass cigarettes hand to hand. Rather like passing marijuana funnel in sadhu *akharas*. Bipasha didn't feel uneasy to sit among them. It was a special experience to read poetry with young and old, known and unknown poets in various neighbourhoods of London. There was no question of invitations; if you came to hear of a reading circle, you could just walk in with poems in your pocket. If there was time, the poems would certainly be read, perhaps followed by thorough discussions. Bipasha would be called to various places by her writer friends. She met the leader of the commune, Betty, at one such reading at Harrington Church. Betty was also a young poet, perhaps slightly older than many, having crossed thirty-eight. She stayed in the commune with her daughter and granddaughter. Her beautiful daughter Cathy did modelling to finance her medical studies, while her fatherless daughter Lisa went to a nursery school. Mother and daughter had two and more lovers who stayed in the commune with them. They were all artists. The commune was very peaceful, neat, and clean. The fridge always had food, the toilets had toilet paper and tissues, and there was no shouting, no affray, no offensive addicts. The residents cooked dinner by turn, and the cooking was done once a day. There was no trace of filthy, negligent, unwashed bodies that the word 'hippy' suggested. All were busy in their work through the day, finished breakfast at their own time, and left in the morning. They came together in the evening, shared their poetry, new songs, and music. Bipasha began to like a boy here. She even considered going to live in the commune. It appeared like a joint family; only, all were young. But the house was full; there wasn't any room free. Still, she kept alive her interaction with Betty. She took Betty's remarks on her poetry seriously.

Betty's young lover was Peter, who was a journalist in Enfield Times and an upcoming poet whose poems were published here and there. Peter, too, was an insightful critic like Betty. Bipasha's poetry improved after listening to their views attentively. The time was around mid 1970s. Salman Rushdie's books hadn't yet appeared, nor had the empire of English fiction overcome the world. In between, Bipasha Choudhury spent six weeks in the Young Writers Colony in Scotland. The manuscript of her first poetry collection was prepared then. Her first book was published by Granta Poetry Society on the recommendation of the mentor of their poetry society, Dame Linda Roberts. The book was received well. *Chequered Sky* also received a small prize for being a young poet's first publication of poems.

This was the time when she began to receive invitations—to publishers' parties, poets' meets at Ireland, Scotland, and Europe. Her life was gradually taking shape—a creative writer's life. She went to Bratislava on one such invitation. She had never gone to Czechoslovakia before. The door had not opened fully then. Ordinary tourists still avoided travelling to the mysterious countries of central Europe. They were busy safeguarding themselves. Bipasha accepted the invitation gladly. The only hesitation was, she would travel to Bratislava and Nitra (*where was that?*), but won't they be taken to Prague? Won't Praha, the centre of Czech social culture, the beautiful and ancient city, show her face to the visiting writers? This was very strange. But Bipasha had no choice.

It was enough that she had been invited. It was like beggar's alms, no scope of choosing.

There was a great distance between the middle-aged Bipasha of today with that Bipasha. When she went to Bratislava, she was twenty-five years old. So was Samir. Bipasha knew that as long as she was in England, Samir was in jail. But who knew which jail? Whether in Purulia jail or Presidency jail, Bipasha had no idea.

Once her entire existence revolved around Samir. Samir was her companion in the failed revolution, Samir was the classmate of her unfinished studies, Samir was the first love of her immature youth. The girl used to speak all the time in her mind with Samir. Year after year. Bipasha couldn't think of herself without Samir. She could never erase the guilt of leaving him helplessly behind to be tortured by the police and seeking a safe shelter for herself. She had never forgiven herself for that. The young woman of twenty hadn't grasped at that critical moment the strategy of her clever businessman father. She was sort of abducted away to Mumbai, using Samir's safety as excuse. By the time she understood what had happened, it was too late for her to undo the deception. They hadn't met after that; neither had they spoken to each other, nor exchanged any letters. She only spoke to herself endlessly; not a discussion, only a one-sided monologue. No answers were forthcoming. Wherever Bipasha went, she took Samir along in her heart. She never went anywhere alone. Samir was always her companion. Nowhere did she go alone. Samir remained with her. Her unfailing companion. Her intimate adviser. Her protector.

Samir was with her in Bratislava. The experience of Bratislava was totally new for Bipasha. She had known only western Europe so far; she hadn't seen eastern Europe. The open competitiveness of capitalism had seemed to her to be the sum total of Western culture. Bratislava made it clear that actually much of Europe remained unknown to her. They went to Czechoslovakia, but didn't step into the Czech region; they didn't see Praha. They returned after getting acquainted only with Slovakia. After reaching there, she found that it was how the workshop had been arranged. In total seven days, they realized that Czech and Slovak were like two neighbourhoods showing the high and low faces of the ethnic culture of the same country. And it wasn't very friendly either. No Czech writer came to their workshop. Bipasha was very disappointed. There was no meeting of minds between Czech and Slovak cultures. Just as capitalist western Europe and socialist eastern Europe had been constructed by contrasting paradigms of value. She had debated this with Johan. Johan's wife was a Hungarian contessa—once Hungary had overflowed with counts and contessas, now they were on the roads—that girl hadn't been able to bear the excessively poor and shackled life of Bratislava and had run away to Paris with her two sons. But Johan concealed that from everyone, even while living alone with his mother. He couldn't even send letters to Paris. Otherwise, the people at the post office would know that his wife and sons were not in Hungary. It was such a small place. All knew that they were with their maternal relatives. Johan was the first secretary of their party's local chapter; it would be highly dishonourable if it became known that his wife had run away to the West. When he could not convince his own wife, how would he explain the ideals of communism to others?

'But Katrina was right to take your sons into the free world. This small, bound country is really suffocating. They can now live under the open sky of Paris. Why don't you too go?'

Bipasha may have said this with a simple mind.

'I should go too?' As though a bomb of combined anger and indignation burst in the room!

'Are you calling capitalism "freedom"? You call that horrible world of competition and envy "an open sky"? Are you mad or don't understand anything? I am working hard all these years believing in an idea. We're trying to create a communist socialist state for our children. Rejecting that idealism, crushing that dream of our future under her feet, that traitor Katrina stole my children saying she was taking them to her parents' home and escaped to Paris. And you are supporting her? Strange!'

Johan was speechless with rage. Then he said, 'Oho, is that because you are a woman? So this is sympathy for another woman? Or is it because you live in a capitalist country yourself? You see freedom for people under capitalism? Oh, actually you won't understand these sentiments. You write poems in English. When, despite living in a colonized country and writing in your native tongue, a countryman of yours won the Nobel Prize, you still write your thoughts and feelings in the language borrowed from the foreign rulers. When you have no bonding with your own mother tongue, how will you gauge the value of my sentiments?'

When Johan told her all this, late in the night, sitting in his empty flat in the flickering candlelight, Bipasha recalled Samir's words when he had tried many years ago to persuade her to write in Bangla. It was very dark outside, lashed by heavy rains and stormy winds without even a flash of lightning. His voice held an odd trace of helplessness. That night, Bipasha impulsively accepted Johan's moment of surrender. She pulled Johan's head on her bosom, as though sheltering a terrified child; no other thought came to her mind. The body made its own decision. Samir was always in her mind. That day of fever. She thought of herself as a traitor. Would Samir understand? When she stood before him again? Would Samir know that Bipasha did not tell Tota's brother about the kitbag? Would Samir believe her? When they met next time? Samir, come and see the kind of wilderness where I exist alone. That boy was still languishing in jail, paying for his idealism.

Some of them had been sentenced for seven years. Those seven years were not yet over. Bipasha made a decision on that rainy night in Nitra that she would return home. She would also try to write in Bangla. Samir, I am now mature enough to keep your word. This insult came from you as before, but not quite as before. This insult is what I deserved. When you are released from jail, you will see that your 'Bi' has returned to you, not as she was earlier, but better and more mature than that. No matter how angry you may be with me, I will melt your anger with my love. Bipasha clearly remembered this like a promise, and uttered this like a pledge on her way back. Her bus was speeding from Bratislava towards Vienna airport. She had calculated mentally: from Vienna to Heathrow, then from London to Kolkata. She must return. How long can she keep running in fear? Samir, will you be able to forgive me?

The other day Bipasha and Anubhav had an argument about language. Even thirty years after that disputation in Bratislava, the same controversy was still alive in India. Mother tongue.

Disha complained that her brother-in-law's son, Anurup, in Delhi was not studying Odiya. He read only English. And since it was taught in school, he knew Hindi quite well but didn't study that either. He was not interested in any Indian language. He read story books only in English. Instead of being worried about this, his parents were actually proud! Anubhav's anxiety was that living in the regionally characterless, cosmopolitan environment of Delhi, his nephew was becoming alienated. He wasn't learning to respect his own culture. He knew nothing of the treasures of the many-sided classical culture of Odisha and its literary resources.

Though his own parents were blithely proud of this indifference, his uncle and aunt were perturbed that the boy was becoming rootless. Arre, this was the same old thinking. This was the way Samir and others thought so many years back, the way nationalists like Johan of that small fighting country still thought. Disha and Anubhav were also thinking like that. In spite of working in such a responsible position placed at the national centre and interacting with different kinds of people all the time, how could they still remain so unaware of the real situation of the country? Bipasha could feel the pulse of the country sitting so far away by merely talking with the American students and the students of the Indian subcontinent. Now, in times of globalization, no one, especially in the developing countries, spared any thought for ideas such as 'mother tongue is mother's milk'. And why should they? The youth will learn the language that will benefit them the most. Anurup wasn't living in Odisha; his father was in Bangalore today, in Delhi tomorrow. What regional language would he learn? Of what use was learning so many languages? He could speak Odiya well, that's it; what more was required? It was obvious that even the chief minister of that state could manage without knowing the mother tongue. One should know the language of power well, the language of success well, know English well. Hindi after that. Anurup had done that. His parents were happy, and rightly too. What language do you use most in your work, Disha? English for writing, Hindi for speaking. Isn't that so? Then how is Anurup at fault? Odiya language won't enjoy longevity in the new world.

Neither will Bangla language, no matter how high Bangladesh flies the language flag. No matter how odious this may sound, one must accept the reality. English alone is our future. There is no other option. But Anubhav continued to shake his head to show disagreement. He didn't accept this. He still believed that mother tongue was essential to sustain your creative identity, or else you were *'na ghar ka, na ghat na'*—belonging neither here nor there, neither at home, nor in the open—a situation that was not desirable for anybody. However, Anubhav's analogy wasn't appropriate in this situation; it was wrong. If Odia was 'home', then English was 'the open space'.

So, if not at 'home', did not the boy already reach the 'open space'?

Yes, Disha knew that her didi, too, had once thought like them, though not so harshly when she returned home after twenty years of leaving the country with a job in a foreign publishing firm. Disha was then a fresh IAS officer. The two cousins met. As adults. Seven years had brought many changes to both. The teenager school student was now a young officer of twenty-two. And the undergraduate from Presidency held a degree from Cambridge, was a prize-winning poet in English, and an editor of intellectual books. They found company in each other for adda at home. All remarked that so many years of living abroad had not changed Bipasha at all. This was the ultimate certificate. But Bipasha herself thought that everything had changed. Everything. Thamma looked as sweet as ever, but had become hard of hearing and walked with a cane. Baba, Jethu, and Jethima had all aged. Borda was in Bangalore with Kaku looking after the office and Chorda was in Texas. Two big televisions sat in two rooms. Baba had exchanged the old car for a new one; Jethu's car was still the same. The cook Balram Thakur, whom Thamma had brought, had gone back to his village; in his place there was a young girl called Renu. Driver Radhanath had become old. The *darwan* Gokul had died. Binoda was still there, ageing and with an irritated mien. All were certainly very pleased to see Bipasha. And young Disha had grown up in these few intervening years. They were now almost of similar age.

Wasn't there a tree here, next to that house, under which we used to sit on the cemented platform? Or, am I making a mistake? Could easily be my mistake. Where did that huge tree go? Was it cut down? Or, wasn't this that house? Isn't this the old turning? Have I come to the wrong place? Several years have passed. How they had laughed when I called the *ashath* tree a *bot* tree. They, from the other *pada*, had better knowledge of plants and trees. There used to be many bushes and shrubs, open ground and ponds in that neighbourhood. Our side had none of that—only buildings, shops, and bazaar, trams, buses, rickshaw, pushcarts, crowded with vehicles and houses. It was still the same. Only the vehicular traffic had increased and there was a jam all the time like the rush hour. There were no horse-driven carts (those weren't there during our days also). The new introduction was the chaotic three-wheeled vehicle called 'auto', and the number of cars had increased to several hundreds. There was no place to walk. I can't imagine driving in this chaos. How did Disha manage? The houses looked dilapidated in our neighbourhood, which seemed to have lost its distinct character. There used to be such old and handsome family homes; right against their walls, unsightly high-rise flats, office buildings, and shops have come up. Old houses were being demolished and replaced by ugly, modern apartment buildings. There was an ongoing contention about our house, too, between Jethu and Baba for that very reason. In one group were Baba, Kaku, Dada, Chorda. Jethima, too, was in their group. For modernization. Thamma and Jethu didn't want the house to be demolished. Disha supported Thamma. Money matters were also a concern. The promoters had offered a substantial sum. Jethu didn't understand business; he had never bothered about it. Baba and Kaku had always run the business. They didn't like Jethu's interference in the matter of business now. Jethu's sons were also in opposition. Even Jethima. Only his daughter was by his side. But, since the signatures of all four were needed, the matter was stuck between the two groups. Her brothers were unhappy with Disha because she wasn't in agreement with them.

No one asked for my opinion. I seem to have been internally distanced from this house. In Disha's view, there shouldn't be any change in Thamma's home during her lifetime. In her opinion, that was the basic and ethical human consideration. Since the house was her property, her wishes should have utmost priority.

Thamma didn't sign when she thought Jethu was right not to sign too. Though the house belonged to all four members, since Dadubhai hadn't left any will, it was actually his property. So Thamma's right was above those of her sons. I thought that all four had equal rights and they should proceed legally. If Jethu and Thamma did not agree, the house could not be demolished. Disha was an IAS officer as well as a district magistrate. She knew legal matters and profit–loss calculations much better. But, for her, Thamma's mental comfort was primary. She was thinking like Jethu. Despite being the youngest in the family, she was on the side of the oldest. The girl attached lot of weight to sentiments.

The more I saw, the more I was amazed. This Kolkata was not known to me. There was so much change among the members of our house. All relations had slowly moved away from each other by a few degrees. I didn't know this Jethima who didn't stand by Jethu's side or of Thamma's, and without following her daughter's advice, she had formed a group with her brothers-in-law and sons staying elsewhere. Dada and Chorda were against Jethu, their father. They supported Baba, Kaku, and the promoters. Did I want to return to this house? Everyone in the house had slowly changed, except Jethu. And Disha had become a totally new full member of the family—this change was welcome.

Had these six-seven years brought such changes within and without that it was now beyond recognition?

Bipasha's first task on returning to Kolkata was to enquire about Samir. She learnt that both Samir and Dipak had been released after five years for good conduct. It wasn't easy to contact old friends to enquire about all. Phone numbers of many had changed. Samir had no phone at home. There was no alternative but to go. She wondered whether to take Rana along; she couldn't muster enough courage to face Samir alone. Who knew how angry he was, how much insult he would heap on her? Police had perpetrated terrible torture on him; his hearing was affected in one ear. Rana said Samir was working for a well-known Bengali newspaper and, ironically, that very paper he and his companions had once set fire to with great fanfare at the street corner, labelling it as an antisocial bourgeois paper. There was no information about Dipak's elder brother. Dipak was working in a school at Khidirpur and was writing notebooks for some publication. After being released from jail, Neela and Ashok had married. They lived abroad. Rana had resumed his MA at Jadavpur University. With Rudrada's help, Ashok had published about three articles in the *EPW*. In Konnagar, Tota's old and helpless parents were spending their very lonely lives. Tota's police brother-in-law didn't permit his sister to visit her parents even now. Tota had died of torture while in police custody and, to circumvent blame, his body was dumped on Red Road. Sometimes, the friends went to meet the parents. But not too often. Who could leave all work and travel that distance so frequently? No, they hadn't taken their responsibility. No one. Diya had a baby girl in prison, Tota's child. It had not been possible for Tota's parents to look after her, so Diya's parents took care of both of them. The child went to school now in Jalpaiguri, and stayed with her grandparents. Diya was working for an NGO in Delhi. Rana was more or less in touch with all of them. Only Bipasha had remained out of touch all these days.

❦

Sokal noy tobu amar prothom dekhar chhotphotani—Not morning as yet, but my restlessness of the first meeting.

After her return to Kolkata, Samir was getting more distanced. Innumerable uncertainties and dilemmas crowded her mind. During the intervening years, living thousands of miles away, Bipasha had been immersed in thoughts of Samir. On opening her eyes every morning, she thought of his unseen face. His eyes seemed to become increasingly more distant. She knew she would fly away like a dry leaf, like a feather, when Samir touched her. Samir would come and stand in the crowd, and the noise and hubbub would be wrapped in solitude and silence. Only the cool breeze carrying the whiff of rain in the distance would caress her face. Bipasha would close her eyes. The city would momentarily be changed by a fairytale magician into an unknown ancient civilization—only in the map of Samir's face would there be a clue to future life.

Bipasha won't waste more time. She felt the chill of uncertainty flow down her spine. Bipasha could no longer stand—her face was held between Samir's palms. With her lowered eyes, she could hear Samir's slow and soft voice descending from the clouds—*Andhokare aar rekho na bhoy / Amar haathe dhako tomar mukh*—Don't let fear fill the darkness / Cover your face with my hands. Then, after that … after that … what would Bipasha do?

Yet, something held Bipasha back. The telephone ringing next door made the blood flush in her chest. She imagined the door bell ringing even as she slept—but where? Where was Samir? Didn't he know that Bipasha had returned? Did he also feel uncertain? Or was he sulking? Had Samir's indignation turned to anger and he was keeping Bipasha away from him? He had captivated her thoroughly, but hadn't she captivated him also?

She won't delay any longer. She had to go. Bipasha made her decision. Samir's newspaper office was located in central Kolkata. She toyed with the idea of taking Rana along. But no, this journey was Bipasha's alone. She would go alone and stand in front of Samir. No one else would be there. Samir's first look—Bipasha wanted to observe his first blink, the indignation in Samir's eyes would pierce Bipasha's being. Then the rain will come and drench the earth.

From morning, she had been thinking what to wear. They would be meeting after so long. Just plain jeans and T-shirt? Samir won't like that at all. He disliked salwar-kurta even more. Bipasha wasn't used to wearing sarees except for parties. But it wasn't as though she didn't wear them. Finally, Samir won; she wore a saree. A pale green and cream combination Sangam print Kota cotton saree—Disha's. The main reason for wearing this was because she had a matching green blouse. She stared at herself for a long while in the mirror, turning this way and that. She liked doing this. She had cut her hair; Samir would immediately comment on that. He had always admired her long hair. She took not a Shantiniketan *jhola* on the shoulder, but a brown handbag of Italian leather, Ferragamo. And matching high-heeled shoes. She had bought the bag from Milan last year. Bipasha uses this bag all the time. Wasn't possible to change the bag; it involved too much work. She paused again in front of the mirror—lipstick? Bindi? She noticed that her nails were painted silvery pink. She thought for a moment and fetched the lipstick and the green Madrasi bindi. She fixed the bindi between her brows with her forefinger touched with vaseline. Checked herself in the mirror again—yes, it was fine, she liked it. Dressing complete. She had no use for jewellery even now. This Bipasha wasn't like the other Bipasha; she couldn't be that again. No one could ever return to the days gone by. Perhaps, she should have gone to Samir as she was, exactly that way. Her innocence, her vulnerability were all known to him. Samir would surely understand. Samir knew her within and without, knew every thought and feeling of hers. T-shirt and jeans would have been fine. That was Bipasha. In a saree, bindi, and ponytail—this was like a dressed mannequin. What would Samir notice? And comment? Lipstick? Bobbed hair? Nail polish? Green bindi? High heels?

Her saree, her short hair, her face with the bindi—Samir didn't look at her at all. Although they looked into each other's eyes while speaking, the eyes themselves did not speak. Samir wasn't surprised to see her, perhaps he expected her to visit his office. He didn't appear pleased. Such anger? But in hiding his rage, dismay, and surprise well, Samir behaved in a strangely formal manner, as one behaved with a little known acquaintance.

As if he was speaking to a neighbour he had suddenly met in the bazaar, 'What, all well?'

Yet, at one point, there was no one in the world who had better understood Bipasha.

Samir addressed her as '*tumi*', but Bipasha couldn't do so. She spoke to him as '*tui*'.

'How do you like working here?... Why did you shave your beard? You look different.'

'I like the work here a lot. I supervise the culture bit. The air of this office carries Bongo-Sanskriti—the culture of Bengal. You will be surprised!' Dismissing the comment on his beard, Samir said, 'What is your plan? Do you plan to stay here or go back?'

The way Samir asked this question, a curtain descended on Bipasha's heart. She could think of no reply.

Samir said, 'Come, let me introduce you to the others.'

It hadn't rained in the city that day. A dense perplexed cloud was settling within Bipasha's heart. She stared at Samir's face and searched for him. Where was Samir?

She met a clutch of people that day who she had known only by their names or by the strokes of their pen. And she saw a completely new Samir. This Samir wasn't surprised to see her; he had already heard of her return. He wasn't happy, nor was he angry. He didn't pretend not to know her. Bipasha hadn't expected this. Samir behaved as though nothing had happened, as though no one had gone to jail, no one had escaped abroad, as though seven years hadn't passed, as though many butterflies flitted around in the yellow sands on the blue ocean shore and children ran about carrying coloured balloons. And they were two strangers—walking side by side. All was well, as was meant to be. The skin colour was fairer than before, not sunburnt; neither was he as thin as he used to be. Yet, his face showed certain exhaustion and age. He shouldn't have shaved his beard, she thought. Bipasha couldn't find the pyjama-kurta clad, thin, angry, bespectacled young man with stubble, wearing sandals, carrying a *jhola* bag on his shoulder, with youthful unshaved face, and absent-minded look in his eyes, who had been her constant companion through these seven years. A stranger had taken his place. Blue- and white-checked shirt tucked into dark trousers, and wearing gold-framed glasses with a thin moustache, he looked smart and very unfamiliar. Samir was wearing shoes and socks.

She looked fixedly at his face and searched for Samir. Where was he?

He talked and joked with his colleagues in a way she found unfamiliar. Had the look in his eyes also changed? Samir was reserved by nature. Bipasha hadn't seen this kind of flippant attitude in him before. He introduced her as a 'famous poet from England, Indian poet in English, and her book has won an award there. I am fortunate that an old friend has taken the time to come to see me.' Full of insinuations, but his colleagues showed immediate approbation. This newspaper was in the habit of respecting poets and litterateurs. Samir ordered tea, black tea with lemon. The tea came with packets of *muri* and peanuts. Samir asked politely, 'Would you like to eat something? There is Anarkali biscuit here ... but will you be able to eat those now?' He spoke with underlying sarcasm. This was the first hint of the past. They used to have tea-biscuits at Ganesh's shop when they were hungry, and Anarkali biscuits were Bipasha's favourite. She hadn't found those biscuits anywhere else other than the tea shop. 'Yes, I can try the Anarkali,' she said and all laughed. 'Oh yes, you won't get those in England!' But she avoided drinking the tea as the glass was dirty. She, of course, said that it was too sweet.

Bipasha wanted to say something to Samir, but couldn't decide exactly what to say. She now knew that there was no single word, no phrase for her want. But Samir's eyes had no sign of any desire to hear anything. There was no solitude in his eyes.

Samir said, 'Come, I'll introduce you to all the seniors.' Wearing a white dhoti-panjabi and seated in a glass cubicle was Santosh Kumar Ghosh. So, this was *Kinu Goalar Goli?* Many sat around the table in front of him. His face showed eagerness to see Bipasha, as appears on the faces of men when an attractive woman enters the room. He asked on being introduced, 'Do you read Bangla poetry? Have you read Shakti Chattopadhyay?' Learning that she had read Shakti, he asked Samir, 'Did you take her to Shakti and Sunil? Take her along and introduce her. Shouldn't she know how the young poets of Bengal now are? What do you say, Bipasha? Even if he is not so young, don't forget to introduce her to Niren. He is also a great poet, right?'

Ramapodo Choudhury sat alone in his room. The other chair was empty. He also wore dhoti-panjabi. He was reading a book. 'What's that book, Ramapododa?'

He raised his sharp eyes and glanced at Bipasha. There was no change in his expression. He told Samir with a slight smile, 'Very interesting. You will like it. It's about the black hole.' He looked at Bipasha on being introduced and asked, 'Have you never written in Bangla?' Sounded rather like a scolding. Bipasha was already feeling guilty. He responded on hearing her answer, 'If you haven't, then you must do so now. Your speak Bangla well! Write prose. Poetry is more complex. Prose isn't easy, but it is the spoken language. Start writing in Bangla now. Can you ever find fulfilment in writing in a borrowed tongue, bhasha that isn't one's own?' Saying this, Ramapodo babu resumed his reading.

The famous poet Nirendranath Chakraborty and writer Gourkishore Ghosh sat in the same room. Not work, they seemed to be having a chat. A long time ago, Gourkishore babu used to be acquainted with a student, Bipasha. He was known to many in their group. Gourda expressed his pleasure to see Samir and cordially invited them into the room. Strange, he met Bipasha after such a long time, recognized her instantly despite her chopped hair, and was aware of every news. He questioned her and seemed to know quite a lot. 'How is your English poetry writing going on? Brought any books?' He introduced her to Nirendranath Chakraborty. But not the way Samir had. He said, 'I know this girl from a long time. Samir's friend and Anupam's student. She studied in England, now she is working there. She has just one fault—she writes poetry in English!' He asked, 'And do you recognize this person? Nirendranath Chakraborty. He is a great poet. But he doesn't write in English.'

Nirendranath smiled, looked at Bipasha, and said, 'Only because I don't, I couldn't become a Shakespeare!'

'But became Niren Chakraborty! Let a few Bongs become another!' Gourda was never short of a repartee.

Nirendranath quickly changed the subject, 'Oh, that's Gour's craziness. Leave all that nonsense. But Samir, did you offer the girl something to eat? Her face looks tired. How long have you been taking her from room to room?'

Sagarmoy Ghosh was alone in his glass cubicle. Samir peeped through the glass and the familiar eyes looked back at him. But they didn't disturb him as he was speaking on the phone. When they returned after a while, he wasn't in his office. Must have left on some work for the day. Bipasha wasn't able to meet him. *Desh* was then the best literary journal in Bengali. The fame of its editor had spread far and wide.

Bipasha was overwhelmed. Meeting so many big names on the same day! Samir's position wasn't a high one at his workplace, but it was clear that he was regarded with affection by all. She couldn't match this Samir, the free and relaxed one here with the shy and reserved Samir she knew. Samir carried on casual conversations with all. Earlier, he used to be free only with Bipasha, that too in private. This person was a stranger to her. Had he changed so much? Does imprisonment change a person so much? Or was this the real Samir? Had the revolution changed him?

She met both Shakti and Sunil that day. Shakti was just as she had imagined him to be from reading his poems; he was exactly like that in his conversation. She found Sunil different. Didn't match. She hadn't imagined him to be so polite and social. She met them later several times on many varied occasions. Rana used to take her to the coffee house at College Street to meet old friends, and had pointed out Nirmalya Acharya and Soumitra Chatterjee to her, but she couldn't meet them. But Samir wouldn't go there. He wanted to go to the coffee house in the office *pada* in Chittaranjan Avenue. Bipasha didn't feel comfortable there; it was dingy, dark, and depressing. It was much better to sit in the Kwality Restaurant at Park Street. Samir was becoming quite difficult. He always spoke to Bipasha with an undertone of sarcasm. He never spoke to her in a straightforward manner; his words always came with a hint of insult. But his humility and courtesy were ever-present for others. Bipasha was becoming impatient.

She happened to attend the *Krittibas* adda on Sunil's invitation. Bipasha would go to various poetry events with Sunil, Shakti, and Tarapodo, and also attended their evening meets over booze. She got to meet the tremendously powerful poets of the 1950s one by one. Some like Shankha Ghosh and Alok Sarkar came to the coffee house adda, but never joined these parties. Alokeranjan was then in Germany. She met Kabita Sinha and Nabaneeta Dev Sen at one such poets' meet. She had never met a poet as spirited as Kabita Sinha even in the literary domains abroad. It was a surprise. Hers was extraordinary and powerful poetry. Rugged yet emotional. She had not met Nabaneeta earlier, but knew about her. Nabaneeta was Sita Chary's friend when she was in Cambridge. The two of them and Sharat Mukherjee's wife Vijaya, who was also a poet, were the three women poets in the literary group she had met. Another woman was writing very well then, Debarati Mitra. But Bipasha never met her. After Sunil, Shakti, Tarapodo, and Sharat, she met Pranabendu and Nabaneeta more frequently than others. Both were teaching at Jadavpur. Whenever she was out for adda with Rana, she went to Jadavpur and peeped into their rooms. Sometimes, after class,

Nabaneeta would drive them and Pranabendu to Maidan, or to the bank of Ganga. They would drink tea in clay cups and chat. They went to meet Kabitadi too at her office in Akashbani. It was wonderful to see her, who, in her poetry, tore asunder the reign of patriarchy and raced in her spirited manner, as a steady and busy government officer carrying the responsibility of her institution on her shoulders. Women knew how to balance their inner and outer lives. Rana had told her, 'Read the writing of your contemporaries, you too would be able to do the same.'

After the 1960s and 1970s, several new and bright minds emerged one after another in the domain of Bangla poetry. By reading their work, Bipasha realized that she was very far away. The fact was, since she had no flair for Bangla language, she couldn't exercise any control over it as she did on English.

Bipasha was changing. She began to think of herself again, transcending Samir. Would she be able to live in this country? Will she? Suppose Samir came tomorrow morning and declared that he was just testing Bipasha, that everything was as before. What if Bipasha saw in his eyes that the temporary smartness had been replaced by anger mixed with resentment? Then? Would she again wait for rainfall? Bipasha felt tired. These past few days had changed her in some ways. She couldn't concentrate on anything. She felt as though a sudden gust of wind could blow away all restraints from her inner being.

Bipasha had become attached to the *Krittibas* poets. She went around with them—Medinipur today, Behrampur tomorrow, Chandannagar the day after; there were always poets' meets. But she went not as a poet but with friends, as a devotee, as a listener. Not even a mad person would want to listen to English poems from a Bengali poet during the later years of the 1970s. No one considered Bipasha a poet. As if writing in English was trivial, negligible, mild. Only Bangla was the language that mattered. Only Bangla could claim respect and honour. Especially after Bangladesh, the pride for the language had increased all the more among the Bengalis.

'Wait, let me introduce you to the Bengali readership, then you will see how many fans you win.' Rana selected three of her poems and translated them into Bangla. He gave them to Samir to get at least one published in *Desh*. But Rana lost his face. Poems by unknown poets were not published in *Desh*. After Samir was unsuccessful with Sagarmoy Ghosh, Rana himself went with Bipasha to submit them to the *Krittibas* editor. Sunil shared a warm relationship with the once-Naxals. He called Bipasha affectionately and said, 'You do read Bangla poetry, don't you? You know Bangla quite well, so what is the need for translation? You are a Bengali girl, why don't you rewrite these poems quickly in Bangla? What you English poets call transcreation. Can't you? You can start right away, I will help you if you have problems.' Sunil did publish them in *Krittibas*. After that, Pranabendu published her poems in *Alindey.* He also sent them to several other little magazines. Bipasha mainly translated or transcreated her poems. Transcreating one's own poems provided more freedom; it was easy to make changes if required. These were not really translations, but recreation 'inspired by' or 'following the shadow of'.

Observing that Bipasha was getting embarrassed over her poems written in English, Rana got determined to take Bipasha to meet Professor Purshottam Lal with her poems. The word 'transcreation' was his coinage. He was one among the early pathfinders for English writing in India. His contribution to anthologizing and publishing such writing was huge. He had encouraged many writers. Professor Lal was then translating the *Mahabharata.* A vast project. He cordially welcomed Bipasha, held *A Chequered Sky* in his hands, and expressed pleasure and encouraged her to continue writing in English. Why should she be embarrassed? In whatever language your pen is free, is your language. No one will come looking for Shakespeare, Keats, or Dylan Thomas in your writing. You shouldn't feel guilty about this. His words gave her peace, but by then, Bipasha had understood that no matter how long she stayed in Kolkata, no matter how many provincial 'little magazines' published her Bangla poems, it won't be possible for her to get recognition as a poet in Bangla. If not for Shakti, Sunil, or Kabita Sinha, she wouldn't even be known as Bipasha Choudhury. No matter how much Rana enthused her, she would not be successful.

One day, suddenly, as they were talking, Samir commented, 'You write in English, you have made a name abroad, you are beautiful, and you have a different glamour. That's why they take special interest in you and print your mediocre poems. Had anyone else written those, those would have landed in the wastepaper basket. Would you call them poems?' About the poems appearing in *Krittibas,* he said, 'Just because Sunilda is a dear and a decent person, he can't behave discourteously with a woman. Otherwise, we know what would have been the fate of a random fellow who approached with such poor quality poems, saying he had come from England.'

Bipasha was afraid of Samir. He seemed to have become rather brutal these days. He was ill-tempered, he was impatient, and he was impulsive—Bipasha knew all this, but she was unable to comprehend what sadistic satisfaction he derived by hurting and insulting Bipasha. Why? She didn't know this Samir, nor was she interested in knowing.

Se ki janito na, ami tare joto jani—Did he not know how well I knew him?

Did Samir never have an inkling about what he meant to Bipasha? About what he was to her? Never?

Bipasha was slowly coming back to herself. She had to separate herself from Samir, or she couldn't live. Bipasha must live. Must keep her sanity. Must hold her own hands firmly. Let Samir remain Samir—Bipasha must learn to be the master of her own soul.

She met Samir from time to time. When free from work, they met for coffee in some restaurant. Mostly Samir spoke; and, in all his stories, his own greatness and his intelligence was demonstrated, or else, he spoke ill of others. Bipasha did not enjoy either of these. Or, they discussed a new foreign film or a new foreign book. But Samir would not talk about his time in jail. Nor would he talk of the old times. He had very few questions about Bipasha; he wasn't interested to know about her life, her mind, and her thoughts—he wanted to know nothing. But she had spent so many years abroad all by herself. Wasn't he curious? Didn't he want to know what friends she had? Whether she missed her home and country? What were her plans for life? Samir had no deep curiosity. Strange! Bipasha had so many things to tell him. But who would listen? Whatever few questions Samir asked were all about her male friends. She couldn't answer freely to this Samir. He didn't trust Bipasha. This Samir kept his heart carefully closed and spoke very cautiously with her. If that door couldn't be opened, then why waste time? Bipasha had also closed the doors of her mind and heart. Samir didn't call her 'Bi' anymore.

The revolutionary consciousness of youth was no longer present in this budding journalist. This Samir sounded super confident, in fact, arrogant. The funny thing was that his arrogance stemmed from his job in a newspaper. If he lost the job, where would he stand with his ego? Had Bipasha returned to this country for this? Whose country was this? She did not know this country. This was not their beloved country, for the sake of whose well-being the youth had sacrificed their future, their lives. The country had also changed. The only good outcome was that there no longer was present the shadow of fear on people's faces. Once again, they could all walk home late after work. The intense violence, the atmosphere filled with inhuman savagery, and the nameless fear lingering in the air no longer haunted this city. Here was Bipasha coming back alone from Behala to Bhabanipur. The evening had already rolled into night. This could not be imagined during the time when Bipasha was smuggled out to England. Whatever is said, Bipasha could clearly see that people were more relaxed now. Violence in the city had reduced a lot.

Many improvements had started to take place during the Left Front regime. Violence had reduced everywhere. Yes, she would visit the villages; she must go. She had taken up a research project on the rural women of a village in Sundarbans near Gosaba. They had visited the region many decades ago on party work at Malopada. They were taken aback, had become restless, and felt an inarticulate pain as they wondered at Nature's vengeance wreaked on the small village. There were many things to be done for them. There were no male members alive there; the village was called Bidhobagram, widows' village. But they could do nothing, as they had other tasks elsewhere to search the neighbouring village for the location and details of the landlord's house. From that time, Bipasha had kept in mind that something should be done for them. Seven years had passed. Who knows how they were? She hadn't been able to visit there after her return. She must make a quick trip before she went back. Disha would surely make all arrangements if asked.

Her mind was becoming increasingly irritated. She wasn't sure how long she could stay here, though she was initially determined to stay.

She didn't quite enjoy passing the evening with her father; that was his time for drinks. If she went to Jethu, he would talk about business and his sons. Thamma only talked about her health and the demolition of the house. Bipasha didn't have a mother; Jethima was Ma. These days, other than the well-loved recipes and food items, she found nothing to talk about with Bipasha. Questions like when she will marry, time was racing by, and that Disha's marriage prospects had become unsettled with her new job—these were her main anxieties and topics of conversation. Or else, the house and the promoters' offers. Disha could be her only companion in this household, but she was very busy with her new job; she couldn't spare much time for her didi. They spoke at night. Very soon, she would get a posting outside the state. Disha was thrilled with her new responsibilities.

Bipasha liked spending time with Rana. He was her companion outside the journalistic and poetic circles. Rana had finally accepted that there was no future here for her poems in Bangla. The place she had found for herself in the world of art and creative writing abroad, she hadn't got an iota of that in her own land. But staying away for long from the sight of readers, editors, and publishers abroad would mean that she could lose that hard-earned place. She must send her work. Professionally, she had no worry because she could easily take a transfer to London with her present job. Why stay here any longer? She couldn't enter the world of Bangla literature. Distance was growing with Samir—did he disrespect Bipasha so much from within? Not just Bipasha, the entire world was the target of his rage and hatred. Although he had initiated Bipasha's introduction with the artistic and literary community here, he himself didn't honour it, but actually scorned it. Morning or evening, whenever Bipasha spent time with him, he invariably expressed resentment about somebody or the other. He described literary community as lacking ideals, opportunistic, greedy, lecherous, self-centred, obsequious, and disloyal. As with all professional lives, he believed the world of professional writing to be tainted with hunger for limitless power. 'One can't see from outside, but there's tremendous competition among them; they are envious of each other. Actually, the whole literary community has no sense of morality. All the money goes for brick-like novels, and poets get token amounts that is almost nothing. No matter how much sloganeering goes on about "*kobiguru*", I know this land has no respect for poetry. In this situation, the little magazines too get wiped out while quarrelling among themselves. Not just the journals, there is lot of power politics among the writers themselves. You can't imagine how far they can go with their pettiness and coterie-making. They don't take women's writing with any seriousness—whether poetry or prose. And is this the case only with literature? The world of art isn't clean either. More horrifying, much filthier is the world of art, a place of greed and gain. There are money games being played, do you know? There is the middlemen's fraud, cases of fake painting and fake sculpture. What isn't there? That world has everything ready for a mystery story. In fact, I feel like writing a mystery novel about them.' Covering the culture bit for the newspaper had given him the chance to observe closely and thus led to his immense disgust with the art and literary worlds.

And the world of journalism? Aren't there political groupism, big schemes of cheating and fraud, and money games too? He cursed others so much, but was silent on journalism. Because he was one of them. The mantra-guru of his youth, Anupam Roy was also a journalist. And a professor. He enjoyed worldwide fame as a bright intellectual. He wrote and spoke with equal calibre. He was celebrated both as a teacher and a journalist. His weekly column 'Roy's Corner' is published even today and circulated from seven cities across the world. But he, himself, has stopped going for lectures because of his voice. Anupam was the first journalist they knew.

Professor Anupam Roy used to lend them numerous books from his own library. He taught them Rousseau's *Social Contract* too. How old were they then? They hardly crossed twenty when Samir was in jail and Bipasha was abroad. Anupam's cowardice was certainly beyond forgiveness, yet there was curiosity to see him if he ever returned to the country. How was his tepid life after the threat of cancer? What were his thoughts? Bipasha wanted to go alone to meet Sir.

Bipasha went with Rana to attend a seminar at the Centre for Social Sciences. Frantz Fanon's writing was being revisited there after a long time. The subject of preaching violence in Fanon's writing, Sartre's views on it, along with Homi Bhabha's objections to Sartre were mentioned in one paper. Many memories were aroused by that small mention. What enthusiasm was there when they had read the book! In the lengthy thirty-page introduction, Sartre had mainly said, 'When they were cornered by abusive consumerism, there was no other way out but violence.' Bipasha had then thought that this perhaps wasn't correct. Was this what Fanon meant? How could Sartre, being Jean-Paul Sartre, write this? Or didn't they grasp the meaning correctly? Was the final message of *The Wretched of the Earth* propagating more violence to protest against violence? Did Sartre make a mistake? Samir and Bipasha had been very surprised. Although young, they couldn't accept Sartre's remarks. Several years later, when Bipasha was studying abroad, there emerged another uproar over this. Harvard's very famous young intellectual, Professor Homi Bhabha, wrote in his essay that Sartre's unilateral introduction had done great harm, and had narrowed down and reduced the vast horizon of Fanon's extraordinary book. Reassured by this, Bipasha thought that all that the elders say may not always be correct. Their immature thoughts hadn't been wrong. Samir only had given her *The Wretched of the Earth* to read in Kolkata. The book had become like the Bible for them. Politically conscious young minds of the 60s and 70s throughout the world considered Frantz Fanon as their spiritual companion. His *Black Skin, White Masks* seemed to offer as if a reflection of the hypocritical and duplicitous mentality of the Indian middle class. One could not not read those two books. That was the beginning of Bipasha's interest in postcolonial studies. She read *Things Fall Apart* after that. Achebe, Fanon—all of them were introduced to Samir by Professor Anupam Roy.

After exiting the lane next to Samir's house, Bipasha walked along the Behala main road, lost in thoughts. Samir's grandmother was alone at home, but she didn't recognize Bipasha. There was no one else at home. The house was the same, yet not quite. The doors and windows had been freshly painted, and the walls whitewashed; it was looking clean. It no longer bore the mark of dire poverty. She noticed a fridge in the inner verandah. Grandma was watching TV, seated on a bed with a clean sheet. She was no longer sitting on a mat on the floor, wearing her glasses to sift rice. Perhaps, her memory wasn't working well. She didn't speak with Bipasha at all, nor asked for her name and so on. Yet, when Samir's brother had died such a horrible death, this same Grandma held the helm of their household in firm hands, consoled everyone, and confronted the police. His father was away from Kolkata; his mother had broken down. Samir had run away. If he hadn't, he would have died that day too. Grandma was a tough lady. How did she become like this? Where were his parents? Who stays at home now? Samir didn't talk about his family. He didn't raise the topic and was uncomfortable if Bipasha did. The moss-covered courtyard had a few flowerpots behind the tulsi shrine. Who had planted those? Big round balls of red fireball lilies. Several had bloomed in the same pot. The dull courtyard was smiling. A yellow-maroon printed kurta was drying on the wire. Whose kurta? She should not have come so abruptly. This was another house, someone else's house. Sunday morning—she had thought Samir would be at home. She would meet his parents. She wanted to surprise them. Who can say why she had wanted this? But nothing happened. No one was at home. Where had they all gone on a Sunday morning, leaving old Grandma alone at home? The fireball lilies in the courtyard seemed to guard Grandma, and the yellow-maroon kurta waved in the breeze like a flag of an unknown country, waving and telling her to keep her distance

Samir was walking with Bipasha, showing her how Kolkata had changed in these seven-eight years. The crowd had increased, as had the number of cars. Minibuses ruled the road—very lawless—speeding everywhere. With the help of the Left Front government, the owners of the minibuses were fattening themselves, and, in a reciprocal gesture, with the help of the owners, the government was fattening itself. Suddenly, Samir signalled a maroon minibus to stop and pulled Bipasha into it. 'Minibus. Dangerous speed. Hold the handle firmly or you will fall when it brakes. This isn't your English bus.' Bipasha was surprised. Where were they going in a minibus? She hadn't felt any warmth in that pull; it was more like an aggression, with a kind of cruelty in it. Like the English 'madam' was being taught a lesson about the ways of the poor country.

They sat down at their old tea shop. It was just the same. There was the shop selling bags just opposite. A man was selling *beli-*

flower garlands next to it. Samir paused for a minute, and then said, 'Should we get some flowers?'

Unprepared, a surprised Bipasha said, 'Yes, I suppose.'

Samir bought the garland and put it on the table. Bipasha, with her short hair, wore jeans and dark round sunglasses. She picked up the garland in her cupped hands and took in a deep breath of the fragrance.

'Some toast and eggs?' He ordered lemon tea and snacks for both of them. He never consulted her about the beverage. Bipasha had noticed, but she didn't suggest coffee for herself.

Samir again asked in the third person, 'So? How does it feel to be back in the country?'

Why the third person? Because there was some solitude here? She avoided the extraneous question and asked, 'Do you meet Professor Roy? Heard he was suffering from cancer … '

No, they hadn't met. After being released from jail, Samir hadn't gone to see him. Although, when in jail, he had felt like confronting him, or knocking thrice on his door at midnight just to see how his ready-witted expression changed. But he hadn't done it. He could never do it. He must have read Samir's articles in the newspaper, must know they were out of jail. No, Rana, Dipak, none of them went. No one wanted to face him. Would he have been able to meet their eyes? When Bipasha returned, he wasn't in Kolkata. He had gone to New York on some UN assignment. Of course, he wouldn't have hesitated to meet Bipasha. Wasn't she of the same group, member of the same kind who followed 'escape to live' philosophy! They got his news from everyone. After his operation for the throat cancer, conversations in his deep, romantic, aristocratic voice had stopped. But, with the help of scientific progress, he wasn't mute. By making a hole in his throat and placing a machine, and with speech training, he got back his voice. He whispered in a low wheezing voice. One could only hear by sitting close to him. He always had a microphone in class. But everyone said that he was not as impressive as before. Illness had changed him, as it certainly would. He had returned alive from the grip of death. As had Samir and his friends.

Didn't any change happen in Samir and others also while they were in jail? He was their main guide, guru, and protector. At least, that is what they thought till that night, when at two in the night, the police raided the tutorial home with the kitbag. All their documents were in that bag that Samir had kept in Anupam's safekeeping. They were arrested together—Dipak, Rana, and Samir. Poor Neela had come that night to look for Ashok. She, too, wasn't left free. But Ashok wasn't there. Bipasha heard everything from Samir. With great rage and resentment, Samir said, 'As soon as the news of our arrest spread, Ashok's uncle took him away to Bangladesh, and your father smuggled you straight to England. Truly, you showed us the reality, you children of the rich!'

Ashok later went to America, where he completed studies and started working. As soon as Neela was released, he came back to marry her and took her away with him. But Neela didn't misunderstand Ashok. They had no problems between them. Then why was Samir so furious with Bipasha? And the language! Was nothing left at all? He continuously insulted her directly and indirectly belittled her. Why should she stay here? For whom? Her father was fine, living happily with everyone at home. He wasn't alone. She had also met Thamma. It was now time for her to return to her place. She had grown no adult roots here.

❦

Kar milon chao birohi?—Whose union do you yearn for, o, lonely one?

It was raining heavily that day. She was supposed to meet Rana and Samir for adda. Then they would have beer and rolls for dinner, as a farewell meeting for Bipasha. She was leaving for London after two days. At one far end of Baghajatin, beyond the wastelands, within a blind lane, was Rana's home of one and half rooms. She didn't find Rana, but Samir was there. Poor Rana had gone to attend a meeting at Uttarpara library; he had gone on his bike and got caught in the tumultuous rain. Samir asked, '*Ki re*, you want beer or whiskey? I am having whiskey.' Today, Samir addressed her as '*tui*'—first time after she came, and when she was ready to leave. Bipasha didn't feel like drinking anything, neither beer nor whiskey. 'Won't you drink anything? You don't care for the local brew, do you? You must have scotch? Then better drink tea. I can make tea for you.' Samir often made tea for them. He was trying to become like he was before.

But Bipasha found Samir, who was trying to be like before, even more of a stranger.

It was not difficult to arrange tea in a small room. Bipasha put the water to boil. Suddenly, Samir spoke in a throaty voice, 'Bi? Will you sing tonight? You had a passion to sing when it rained.'

Did Samir call her 'Bi'? He hadn't said that even once all these days. But why didn't Bipasha feel any thrill? Samir was asking her to sing. Earlier, whenever they met, they spent their time singing. They didn't sing anymore in their addas, she had noticed. Bipasha felt that they had no joy, that all had become strangely old. Instead, Sunil, Shakti, and others were much better. When the night became softened with alcohol, they started to sing heartily. Bipasha's singing voice wasn't bad, she only lacked practice. She didn't have much contact with Bengalis in England. Her life and profession had sort of fixed her in the English environment. Who would she sing Rabindra Sangeet to? She listened to music in her own room, and sang to herself.

'After my stay in England, I don't have the typical Bengali sentimental attachment to the rainy season, Samir. No one could, really. Drizzling the whole day, the sky and earth all moist and soggy, monotonous and dull. Rainy season has lost that romantic status for me. Songs have also disappeared from my life. My song won't be like before.' Nevertheless, Bipasha sang a song for old times' sake. Not specifically a song of rain. But, in this liquid darkness, with the steady sound of rains, a melody struck her heart and went on pounding her like waves. It was in *shree* raga, calm and deep. Bipasha closed her eyes and sang with all her heart: 'Whose union do you yearn for, o, lonely one?'

Bipasha felt Samir's hand on her cheek as she sang. Not Samir's hand, but the hand of a man. Samir's hand seemed rough, unfamiliar. Like a blind person, Samir too was trying to recognize by touching something found after a long time. He was trying. The suffocating humidity after the rains settled on Bipasha. She continued to sit where she was. Samir's masculine hand became restless. Bipasha seemed to know its movements. Samir's breaths made hissing sound. But Bipasha wasn't afraid. She was thinking something else and remained sitting as she was. Now Samir kneeled in front of her and, like an algebraic formula, pushed the saree away from her breast. Like an immature adolescent, Samir was rubbing his head on her breast. Bipasha recalled Johan. Samir's hair exuded a dank smell, like moist garments in the rain. Bipasha's eyes remained open with a faraway look. Samir placed his wet lips on hers. Bipasha felt suffocated. Slowly, she pushed Samir away. He grasped Bipasha's body with his arms. He was trembling. But Bipasha was no longer with Samir; she was far away. Her brows met—she was thinking.

At that moment, she felt that this was no longer a game with her own misunderstanding. She must go back. She must write in English. Bipasha must return.

Samir tried to kiss her again. Failed, Bipasha had moved her face away. The sultry humidity in the room became unbearable; Samir grew impatient. He unbuttoned his shirt with one hand; Bipasha watched with calm eyes as Samir tried to pull her closer towards him. She felt the touch of his arrogant physicality. Samir now tried to embrace and lift her on his lap. His breath held the threatening sibilance of endless hooded serpents. Still, Bipasha wasn't afraid. She felt tired. She tried to push Samir away a little. He stopped her. Bipasha pushed harder to free herself and said in a calm normal voice, 'Enough.'

Samir whined in a begging tone, 'Please Bi, don't do this.'

Bipasha appealed too, 'Please, no.'

Samir sounded distraught, 'Can't you understand my condition?'

Bipasha understood. Lifting her *anchal* back, she said, 'Go to the bathroom.'

Samir's eyes burned with rage. Poison dripped from his raised serpent hood. He cried, 'Why? *Satitva*, purity? Is it?'

Bipasha's eyes glistened in amusement, 'If I say yes, then?'

Samir was enraged, 'Stop making fun of me.' He grabbed Bipasha's shoulders and tried to pull her close by force.

Bipasha giggled. '*Dhur*, the role of a rapist doesn't suit you. Let me be.'

Samir grabbed her shoulders with the claws of a savage beast, tried to force her into his lap, and said in an unfamiliar growl, 'That's what you say. All this *satitva*, purity, for me, no? You think I don't know how many men you've slept with?'

Bipasha wasn't afraid. She shook herself free of Samir. 'Go away.' She moved Samir's greedy hands away like insects from her body. 'There is no need for you to count yourself among those men.' Bipasha straightened her clothes and got up.

She felt calm and at peace. The new Samir resumed his normal state. For a little while, he had been trying the mask of the old Samir to frighten her.

Bipasha stepped out in the rain. She regretted wearing a saree even when she knew that heavy rains were forecast. She wore sandals to go with the saree. It would have been much easier if she had worn jeans, T-shirt, and running shoes. She stared at the mast light at the bus stop like a lodestar; she would have to wade through the dirty puddles in the darkness. The unlit, blind lane seemed pathless, endless. Stepping very cautiously on the higher edge of the road, she reflected in surprise. When Samir came close to her body, why hadn't she recalled their first kiss on the dark steps of the tutorial home even once? Why hadn't she thought of that afternoon when Samir was down with fever? Or, of Johan's desperate face?

Well, it was now time to return. In the heavy rains, Bipasha suddenly felt herself to be burden-free, guilt-free, independent, and fulfilled.

Rohini

Rohini Bettina Anderson was born in a small hospital in Greenwich. Bettina was George's mother's name and the name Rohini was given by her father. If it was a girl then 'Rohini', if a boy then 'Rohan'. A head of curly black hair, white skin, and rose-petal lips, the baby looked just like the fairytale Snow White. But this wasn't a fairy tale. This baby had spoilt Bipasha's body, had torn through her arteries to make an appearance. She was made with her blood and flesh from the most interior part of her body. There, in God's miraculous workshop, she had grown for ten months. How did all this happen?

Bipasha had made a mistake in counting days. They didn't remember. If George was thrilled and excited to learn that he would be a father, Bipasha was sad and quiet. In his delight, George married her thinking of the baby's future. Though not very pleased, Bipasha didn't object to becoming Bipasha Anderson. The future of an unborn person would depend on her decision. It was no fault of the child.

But should Rohini be told the truth about her birth? … 'So that she never has to suffer in her life as I did, I told her everything when she was thirteen. I was totally honest with her,' Bipasha declared with pride.

Bidisha looked the other way. Lines of dissent crossed her face. She seemed to be thinking. Bipasha felt hurt somehow. She needed concurrence at this moment. Sometimes, the lack of agreement disturbed her. 'I was honest with my daughter, Disha.'

Bidisha smiled sadly. 'Honest? Doesn't this carry the smell of postcolonial intellect, Didibhai? What would you call this—theoretical honesty?'

Bipasha realized that her little sister had become her equal in age. She will be crossing fifty soon. So she can't expect unconditional support. Suddenly, Bidisha looked into her eyes and said, 'Who gained what from this honesty, Didibhai? She wasn't the child of her mother's love, but the fruit of an accident. How did this knowledge benefit the girl? The foundation of her trust must have been shaken forever, wasn't it?'

'But I ensured that she was not wanting in anything, Disha. You have seen this. Didn't she get any support from me?'

Bidisha didn't speak, only smiled a little. Bipasha knew that her smile held contempt and a subtle insult. Bipasha was feeling weak. After this, staring at her eyes like throwing a challenge, Bidisha said in a calm and cool voice, 'Okay Didibhai, what did you tell her? That she was the loveless child of yours? But not George's, right? Did you tell the girl this separately? With honesty?'

Bipasha guessed that her mind was undergoing a huge upheaval. From her sister's scornful comment, a precious perspective became clear to her. She, at last, found freedom from a very old and acute sense of non-acceptance. It was true that the child was not hers alone. She was also her father's child. And her father was, from the moment of her birth, totally devoted to his daughter. Whatever was her mother, whatever was her own incompleteness, Rohini hadn't experienced any lack of welcome from the moment of her birth. Yes, she had not told the right thing to her daughter. Rohini's birth wasn't loveless, nor was her growing-up years. So much so, George's wife and sons had loved Rohini and she had loved them back. Then, was she the excluded one? Did motherly love not flow in her bloodstream?

Rohini did her graduation in film studies. The film she made for her exam was exceptional; George saw it. After that, Ro had made a documentary on the Bangladeshis of Bradford. Bipasha heard that it won a prize in a documentary film festival. Rohini was a film journalist initially; now she is a filmmaker and screenplay writer. She has already made a few popular ad films, besides writing several screenplays for BBC Channel Four. Rohini is now standing on her own feet. She has started a production house with two of her friends. Sometimes, she wrote short stories too. George informed Bipasha of his daughter's achievements with pride. Endless distance kept growing between the mother and the daughter day by day.

As a girl who had lost her mother, she received extra love and attention from her father, as from others in the family. Bipasha never felt the absence of a mother, nor any emotion and sentiment over the loss of her mother. How could she miss someone she had never seen? No, she never missed her mother. In fact, there had grown in her a kind of disinterest about the concept of motherhood. Her maternal grandmother used to call her 'mother-devouring girl'. Thamma said, 'Ah, your mother longed for a girl and she did get a daughter. But the poor thing never got to see her face.' Jethima said that it was the beginning of her father's drinking habit. He would sit with a bottle in the evenings, as he had become lonely. But why did they say all this to her? What could she do? Did Bipasha have anything to do in this? If someone departs from the world while bringing her into the world, why should she be held responsible for that misfortune and bear the guilt throughout her life? An inexplicable fear built its home in her mind. Why should she become a mother? Why should she put at stake her body, time, labour, pain, and lifespan to make another being see the light of the world? Why should she be bothered? She hardly cared. Bipasha wasn't fond of children. No, she never harboured any wish to be a mother. But, looking at Rohini, a vague anxiety floated into her innermost heart; she had repaid the debt of her grandmother by bringing another girl into the world.

But why was Rohini coming to Bipasha after so many years? What was she thinking of? What did she want from her mother?

Surely, she had nothing to learn about child-rearing from her. She smiled at this ridiculous thought. Then? She has adopted a child—that would incur some expenditure. Was it easy to bring up a child? Her income was irregular as she held no regular job. But George possessed more than enough wealth, in the bank and in his heart. He was devoted to his daughter. Rohini would not face any monetary shortage. Then? Was she bringing her adopted child so far to show her to Bipasha? Out of affection of her heart? Bipasha could have easily travelled to England for some reason or the other and seen the baby. Or wasn't the matter so simple? The mother who couldn't give her enough care and affection, and admitted lack of love, was Rohini trying to teach that mother what love was? That it wasn't necessary to bear a child for that? One could be close to another in different ways. Was Rohini coming across the Atlantic to tell her this? Was she coming to say, 'Ma, see, you pushed away your own. I have made the distant my own.' Was Bipasha upset with all these thoughts?

'Don't worry at all, Didibhai, I'm going to the airport. I will take care of everything. You go to the meeting peacefully and return as the president! All the best.'

Bidisha was glad to pick up Rohini and her child. In Delhi, she spent her days engrossed in numerous official duties. Here it was like a holiday, with sufficient time for her studies. She hadn't seen Rohini for many years after her childhood. Then they met at Delhi when Rohini came on some film-related work for which she had to connect with the government. She stayed with her aunt. Anubhav was the joint secretary of Culture, and could offer useful suggestions. He helped her make many non-governmental contacts and assisted her in many ways. She had spoken at great length with Aunt and Uncle about her work and life in general. Both Bidisha and Anubhav had liked Rohini very much. She was no more the problem child that Didi had described. May be, she had been once as a child, but was no longer. Now she appeared quite mature, intelligent, and a compassionate girl. This time, she had something extra to offer. Bidisha was very eager to see the baby. They knew her life story. Rohini found her in a village during the making of a documentary. She always had the tendency to do, at the drop of a hat, whatever her fancy took her. The habit her mother always complained about. This was proved in the matter of adopting the baby.

For quite some time, she was planning to shoot a film in India. She received sufficient help from NRIs in England. There wasn't any worry about finance. What was now needed was the solution for a number of problems that a foreigner faces while trying to make a film in India. She had the necessary visa to work in India; now small legalities had to be solved along with permissions. That required locally available and dependable crew, local actors, DOP, sound engineers, lightmen, camera hands, and so on. A good line producer could get all these things together. Anubhav had helped Rohini with that. Working in the Ministry of Culture for a few years had brought him into contact with different sorts of people.

Rohini's core team was from England. Main camera, sound, music, and editing would be handled by her English team. The principal role was of a woman. For that, there was a foreign artiste, Nina Jha. She spoke English, Bengali, and Hindi well. The daughter of a Bengali mother and Bihari father, she was born and brought up in England. She was now working on crossover films. It was she who had arranged the financier. The producers were two non-resident Indian businessmen. They too were very interested in crossover films. Indian actors would be needed for the other roles. Arrangements were getting done slowly. The film would be shot partly in the village, partly in the city. The local team was travelling to villages in West Bengal to decide which sections would be shot in which locations, where local help was readily available, who should not be angered, who needed to be buttered, etc. Anubhav had also managed to get her a canny boy who could handle these matters. Rohini had started work with concentration. The film had progressed also when it was time for Bidisha-Anubhav to leave for Boston. Rohini wasn't living at a stretch in India, but was travelling to and fro intermittently. By the time Bidisha left, her assignments in Delhi were more or less done. Rest of the work would be done in Kolkata and its suburbs, majorly in the Sundarbans.

In Kolkata, Bidisha introduced Rohini to Bipasha's father, her uncle and aunt on the phone, 'This is your maternal uncle's house, *mamarbari.* Throughout the world, all Bengalis get maximum spoiling in this one place, *mamarbari*. Your share of that remains untouched, don't miss it.'

No, Rohini didn't miss '*mamarbari*'. Bipasha's daughter received great love and care. She was the closest to Bipasha's father and uncle, as if the two grandfathers had got Rohini in Bipasha's place. Jethima phoned Bipasha several times and told her this. They were all impressed with Rohini's behaviour. Rohini endearingly called them Dadubhai, Jethudadu, and Jethididu. She ate rice mixed with *shukto**, and carefully picked the fine bones from the *ilish maach.* She wore the saree they had gifted her so well and came to show them. She was looking elegant. All the discussions about Rohini had the phrase '*ki sundor*'—how beautiful—from Jethima. The last comment was inevitably, 'Ah, your thamma didn't get the chance to see her!'

Rohini had won them over magically.

'Listen, Tuku, your daughter is lovely. Looks just like you, her face and smile. Her aunt's height, added to that, the white skin like her father, and black curls like her Dimma. Most beautiful is our granddaughter. Her behaviour too is so sweet; she speaks with the servants sweetly and in broken Hindi. Just like you, grabbing

---

* A traditional Bengali dish prepared in mustard and poppy seed gravy.

affection by her nature. But now that she is of marriageable age, you must think of her marriage. The only problem I have is in language. I can understand what she says, but can't make her understand all that is in my heart. I can't manage English that well, can I?' The girl wasn't staying at home. She, with her crew, stayed in a hotel out of courtesy. Bipasha was surprised that Jethima made no complaints about that. Everyone had changed there.

Bipasha thought Rohini would be happier to see her aunt and uncle at the airport rather than seeing her. For her, Ma didn't mean comfort, Ma didn't mean taking rest and returning hale and hearty. In Rohini's life, Ma meant bitter arguments, Ma meant conflict. Bipasha understood this much. Now she was coming as a mother herself. This child was fully a child borne of love. Wherever the baby had come from, if not in her body, this mother had taken it into her heart; this mother, Rohini, had given birth to the child anew in her lap. Dependent on this mother's affection was the well-being of the child's bones, skin and flesh, and happiness. How did the baby look? Boy or a girl? Skin colour? A strange curiosity was growing in Bipasha's mind and an eagerness for the yet unseen child of her daughter. Although she has never liked children.

Would Bidisha over-enthusiastically take them out for dinner, thinking that she was busy in the meeting? As it is, there would be jet lag, plus with an infant, there should be some rules.

It was very late when Bipasha returned after finishing the meeting and the dinner. The decision was declared at dinner—her attendance at the meeting was successful.

The first good news was that that was the first time an Indian had become the president of the Association of Postcolonial Studies (IAPCS); the second good news was that she was the first woman president. The vice president was Princeton's Professor Marnoff. This, too, was a good news. David was an old friend from Harvard, her own person. She got what she wanted, but there was no peace in Bipasha's mind. Hope Rohini wasn't feeling neglected—oversensitive, as she is. Hope she wasn't angry? She was coming to her mother after so long, and the first time with her baby, and her mother was in a meeting? '*I am always the second preference for my mother.*' It was her nature to be angry. But what was the use of worrying? What she did was right; she had made the correct decision. Everyone lived their own life. The day had been full of tension. She felt exhausted. Disha had messaged the news of their arrival; she said she must drop at their place on her way back.

No, she won't go to meet them so late in the night. They will anyway come next morning. She would explain everything after they came. If they understood, fine; otherwise she was helpless. This relationship of misunderstanding had gone on with her all through life. When wasn't Rohini angry with her mother? The following night, too, she had a meeting—the farewell banquet of the conference. Bidding goodbye to the old committee and welcoming the new one. The newly elected president must preside at the banquet. Bipasha would have to leave them in the evening. She could miss the conference the whole day, but should not miss the banquet. Her first responsibility after becoming the president was to bid farewell to the former president. She would have to write a short, striking speech.

Bipasha would have to wangle out the time from Rohini and her child. She would again have to burden Disha for tomorrow's dinner; there was no option. She had run through the matter of the banquet in their hearing. There was enough food at home; she had to only warm them up. Overwrought in her thoughts, Bipasha put down her bag, removed her shoes hurriedly, and, before changing her clothes, phoned Bidisha.

Bidisha was very excited. She spoke non-stop as soon as she picked up the phone.

'I'm sure, Didibhai, you got it? Am I right?'

Bipasha smiled in a controlled way, 'Hmm, it was done.'

'Congratulations, Didibhai! Gr—ea—t news! We knew it!'

'Thank you, *re*.'

'Now listen to the real news. I mean we knew yours already. You deserve it. But your daughter has made a scandal,' Bidisha's voice held adolescent excitement.

'Scandal? What has she done?' Bipasha's voice sounded tired after the day's work.

'Oh, that's so big! She is very disappointed that she couldn't meet you.'

'She is always disappointed with me. Leave it, how's the baby?'

'You won't believe it, Didibhai. I mean this is very strange. But she looks exactly like our thamma. There's no reason, but … ' Her excitement wouldn't stop. Bipasha smiled.

Disha acted so crazy sometimes, really! You hold such a big job. Bipasha grinned.

'You don't believe me? Well, you'll see for yourself. Can't tell you how sweet she is. She clings to her mother, but accepted us too. Came to my arms without any hassle. And Rohini? Oh, my god! She is such a wonderful mother! Imagine, that little girl—'

Bipasha didn't respond. Rohini was twenty-eight. At that age, she—

'At least, that mad hatter girl has some restrictions now.'

'Can you call her to the phone?'

'Oh, haven't given you the real news! But Rohini has fallen asleep … I mean she was very tired with the baby, so a little while ago … '

'That's okay, I understand. But what's your real news?'

'Really, I've lost my mind, Didibhai! Do you know what your daughter has done? You can't imagine. A huge surprise!'

'What has happened?'

'Her film has gone to Cannes! Didibhai, to the Cannes Film Festival. Can you imagine? Can't believe it, can you? Such success with her first feature film! This film is having a big world premier show in New York. She is going there tomorrow.'

Bipasha was astounded, but said, 'Going tomorrow? When?'

'Oh, Didibhai, haven't told you yet. You can't meet them tomorrow. That's why I asked you to drop by tonight. They must leave early morning tomorrow.'

'Is it? Leaving early morning?'

'She must reach New York tomorrow. The premier is tomorrow. A huge event. Can you guess how many festivals her film will go to? Surely Cannes, then Venice, Berlin, Toronto, and some more places.'

Bidisha was speaking like an overflowing fountain.

'It's a great achievement, Didi.'

'Great news, indeed, very good news.'

'Good? We're going insane with excitement. Anubhav too.'

Bidisha was not by nature so excitable. Her enthusiasm made Bipasha a little surprised.

'Is this the film for which in India … '

Interrupting her, Bidisha said, 'Yes, yes, that one. The one I told you about. That film. You were thinking why Rohini was coming. She came for this. After such great success and wonderful news, your daughter was coming to meet you. Such a nice girl she is in every way, just think … '

'If she leaves early morning tomorrow, then how will she meet me?' Her voice was cold, controlled.

'She will return in a few days, after the premier and the press meets. Oh, listen, Didibhai, shall I say something?'

'What?'

'Anubhav and I have already bought our tickets; we're going to New York with her. We'll stay for the premier. When does one get such a chance for a big celebration?'

'You too are going?'

Bipasha was surprised.

'Arre, George and Eileen are coming too. It's a great thing. Didibhai, why don't you come too? The girl will be so thrilled.'

'I? But … '

'When will you get such an opportunity, tell me? Our Rohini will surely make many more films, but this is her first film after all. The girl's first picture is getting such a huge world premier show in New York; such moments come once in a lifetime. It's very important for you to be present. Think this over, Didibhai. Will you come with us?'

'Arre, I have that banquet tomorrow. How can I go? You know this, right? I'll watch that on a DVD later. But this is great news, really! I still can't believe!'

The excitement in Disha's voice was now replaced by a hint of complaint, 'George and Eileen can come from London. You are her mother, can't you go to New York from Boston? At your daughter's world premiere?'

'You know this Disha, my banquet was fixed many days ago.'

Bidisha said quietly, 'Didibhai, I think she came to take you along. Otherwise, she could have flown directly to New York. Isn't it? She would have finished all matters and then come to Boston. Why did she take so much trouble to come here to you for a day with her tiny baby?'

Bipasha was in difficulty.

'But Disha, you don't understand. It's my duty as the new—'

'Sorry Didibhai, I was making a mistake. It's alright.'

'*Byas*, you're angry!'

'Why should I be angry? Our priorities are different. That's all.'

'See Disha, you are now accusing me. I would have certainly gone had it been any other day. But, about tomorrow evening, I am helpless, I'm duty-bound.'

'Okay, Didibhai. Duty-bound! All the best. I must go to sleep now, have to get up early tomorrow morning.'

'Listen Disha, you—'

'Sorry if I was rude. By the way, I forgot to tell you in all the excitement. Rohini had many radio and TV interviews about this film. The papers also carry preview. Rohini has brought along some interviews and paper reports in a CD to show us. I kept the CD in your letter box. If you can look through them. You will know many unknown details about the girl; she had also said many things about you. Goodnight.'

Bidisha disconnected the phone.

It was good that Bipasha hadn't yet changed her clothes. She slipped on her sandals and ran downstairs. Let's see in which interview her daughter has talked nonsense about her mother. Surely, nothing good. It wasn't little trouble she had taken to bring up her daughter. Rohini's childhood wasn't easy, and Bipasha's career was just taking shape. She couldn't give the amount of attention needed to be given to either. To be attentive about her career meant being attentive about her future, and along with that was Rohini's future. She had a long span of time to grow up, she had a lot of time. But how much time did Bipasha have? George got a fifteen-year-old grown-up daughter. There was not one, but three-four newspaper interviews and a CD. The first interview she opened carried a full-size picture of the girl. Very impressive, indeed. Such height already ensures plus points. And she has a great figure, and long hair covering her.

She put the papers on the table, changed into her nightwear, and cleaned her face for a very long time. She lightly massaged anti-ageing nourishing cream over her face and throat, took her medicines for the night, combed and arranged her hair properly, and then took time to gently massage anti-wrinkling beauty milk on her arms, legs, and chest. Staying for long in thermostat-controlled rooms dried, roughened, and wrinkled the skin if proper care was not taken. These fell in her daily duties. No matter how tired she was, she never neglected this task. Bipasha looked at herself in the mirror and seemed satisfied. She then took a long glass of ginseng tea with ice cubes, picked up the interviews, and sat in the armchair with them. All lights in the room were switched off other than the bedside reading lamp. Today had been very strenuous, though she had to do nothing. She didn't even have to give a speech. Her speech would be tomorrow. If they didn't come tomorrow, then she would be free. She would go to the conference. Before that, she must write the farewell speech for Professor Bighnaraje. He was truly a nice person, though he may not be a good theorist. Much research was going on at his centre on multicultural studies. Placing her feet on the footstool, Professor Bipasha Anderson picked up the first interview.

'Anderson Makes Waves.'

The very headline passed through her like a lightning current.

She lowered the paper and sat stunned. But something was stirring in the depths of her feelings. Her eyes stared unseeingly at the light beige colour of the walls—an image of the bright white walls of the Greenwich Hospital rose before her. A cradle. Bipasha lowered her eyes again on the paper. The full-size photo. Rohini was smiling.

She thought of something, put the papers aside, pulled the laptop, and inserted the CD.

A TV interview was starting. Rohini was facing the sharp questions from a star BBC journalist. A sixty-minute-long conversation.

'Good evening, Ms Rohini Anderson. I welcome you to this discussion forum. Heard that your film is going to the Cannes Festival? Hearty congratulations.'

'Thanks. Yes, that's what I heard too,' she smiled.

'For a young director's first full-feature film to be invited to Cannes Film Festival is a great honour, an instance of unprecedented success. One must say this—'

'Yes, that's right. I consider myself very lucky—'

'Weren't you greatly surprised, too? Did you expect this much?'

'Um, to tell the truth, I am happy but not surprised. If I didn't think at all that a call might come, would I have tried to send it to Cannes?'

'You seem very courageous.'

'You can say that. For artists to work, isn't a certain degree of courage necessary?' she again smiled.

'Do you believe yourself to be an artist?'

'Certainly, I do. History will decide if that art is good or mediocre, but whatever I create, I create as art.'

'Yes, art reminds us. You are also a young litterateur. In literature, your main area is fiction. Has anything other than your short stories come out? Have you begun any novel?'

'No, I want mainly to be a film-maker. Novel is not my form.'

'Your mother is a poet. Haven't you tried your hand at poetry?'

'No, I sometimes write short stories, that's all. I don't have ambitions in literature. My thoughts, imagination, planning, and labour are meant to be used for films.'

'Do you regard yourself as a feminist film-maker?'

'Yes, you could say that. I regard myself as a feminist film-maker. At the centre of my art is woman.'

'Who do you consider your ideal director or directors? And who is your role model?'

'There is no one in front of me as a role model of an ideal director. For different reasons, I have liked the work of different directors. Among the classics, Kurosawa, Bergman, and Satyajit Ray are definitely there. Among the recent, Wong Kar-Wai, Kim Ki-duk, Majid Majidi … '

'But they are all men. You say you are a feminist film-maker. Why don't you proceed with a woman film-maker as role model?'

'A woman director doesn't always mean a feminist director. Free of the "male gaze" in their work cannot be said of many women film directors. Both here and internationally, there are many women directors, but their perspective is not that of a woman. On the other hand, there are male directors who have borrowed the female point of view and are making feminist films. These days, several powerful women directors have come. I respect their way of looking and their perspective. Women's film festivals have become very influential these days. Strong feminist films are coming from otherwise weak countries—'

'Despite that, you didn't find a single woman director in your list of ideal directors?'

'See, the matter of point of view is one thing, while matters of film-making like expertise, creativity, and construction of a film are different. A film-maker's excellence is judged, taking all these aspects into consideration. I do not wish to bring gender discrimination in the matter of judging excellence in film-making. All artists are equal. You have to select the best.'

'Do you think what you're saying now keeps your feminist-model sacrosanct?'

'Certainly, it does, I think. There is no contradiction between the two. Anyone who makes a good film will be my ideal. Gender discrimination doesn't work here. Feminism is a philosophy of life. Film-making is artistic and a technological skill. It will be my personal task to make the two meet in my work.'

'Fine. Which woman director would you like to be placed beside?'

'I think that to distinguish excellence according to gender in any field of art is showing disrespect to women's genius. The area of our competition should be open and generous, and the way to learn should also be unrestricted. If women compete only with women, will they also learn only from women? Do women live in a separate women's world?'

'Interesting reaction. In this connection, it comes to mind that lesbianism has become essential to feminist films. What are your thoughts on feminism and lesbianism? Is there any lesbian angle in your film?'

'There is an important place for gender politics in every film. But to say this has become redundant now. Feminist angle is not necessarily a lesbian angle. Every feminist film need not to be a lesbian film. I think excessive pressure of lesbianism in works of art is not helping feminism. Instead, this is creating a huge area of misunderstanding. It is making the sky of feminism very narrow, very limited.'

'This is worthy of thought. Let us move away a little. Will you classify this film as a crossover film?'

'Surely, it will be.'

'Then Gurinder Chadha, Mira Nair, and Deepa Mehta are remarkable directors of crossover films. There are other such feminist directors. In India, there is Aparna Sen. Are you indebted to any one?'

'Absolutely. All of them are important directors, without doubt extraordinary. I respect their work. Their work may have influenced my film. That is but natural.'

'That's good. Can you briefly say what is the basic message of feminism in your film?'

'Not just empathy for women. Basic to feminism is to oppose violence against women, and violence per se, in society. I am against all kinds of violence. If that opposition becomes violent, I will be against that too. This is why I don't support militant feminism, don't support any kind of terroristic revolution. I believe that feminism doesn't support the slogan "violence against violence". I have tried to show this in my film.'

'Who are your ideals for feminism?'

'My ideal for feminism was always and still is Gloria Steinem. Another is Germaine Greer. My thoughts match theirs to a certain extent, but not entirely.'

'Luce Irigaray?'

'No, French feminism is different than ours in its way of thinking. I don't think like Luce Irigaray.'

'Your mother Professor Bipasha Anderson is famed through the world for her views on postcolonial feminism. She once worked with Gloria Steinem for a magazine. She edited books from the Feminist Press with Florence Howe. She is very free in her own life. Such a person can easily become a role model for any modern woman. But you didn't mention your mother?'

'Yes, my mother has done useful work with feminism. My mother's work on postcolonial feminism is pioneering. Ma is feminist in her own way, I am in mine. Times have changed; the perspective of two generations cannot be the same.'

'Your father is British and mother Indian. You spent some time of your life in America and some in Britain. Which country would you say you are a film-maker of?'

'I think of myself as a British-Indian film-maker. I grew up in America, it's true, but in my blood flow Britain and India. I am, to a large extent, Bengali due to my mother's influence. My film, too, is like me, British and Indian. And to a large extent Bengali.'

'What is this film about?'

'This is the narrative of some educated Indians who live and have settled in Britain; side by side, with their lives, are people of rural India who are severely underprivileged. This is the story of existence, of trying to live. Of a village that became prey to social, political, and economic multipronged violence, about women of that village, and about a village of widows in West Bengal. No men are alive in that village. Just as there is a mixture of the two cultures of Britain and India in the pages of my short story, it is the same in my film.'

'Would you call yourself an Indo-British film-maker or an Indo-British writer?'

'Sure. I can surely be called an Indo-British craftsman.'

'Your mother is also a famous Indian writer in English. Is your mother your role model in the matter of creative writing?'

'No, I cannot call my mother my role model. I am a prose writer, while my mother is a poet. Her talent is in poetry; she never wanted to be a fiction writer. My mother's prose means her essays; in that she is a world-famous intellectual. Postcolonial literary theorist. I am a film-maker by profession, an ordinary short-story writer. I am not an academic. How can I make my mother my role model? Neither of us likes the other.'

'What do you mean?'

'Many things about me are not liked by my mother. There are many things about my mother that I don't like.'

'Meaning? Give an example.'

'I mean that in comparison with my mother, I am more traditional.'

'Conventional?'

'Yes, our generation is AIDS-sensitized and self-controlled, a cautious generation. Mother's generation spent a much more liberated and unbound life. She was a student during the unrestrained 1970s. She did a lot of experimentation and examination with her life. She participated in the revolutionary student politics in India, had practical experience of the violent agitations, and she escaped from the police and came to England. Her companions were sentenced to seven-year prison; she would have been similarly jailed had she been caught. In England, she spent countless days with hippy artists. It had its benefits. She supervises worthwhile research, does serious work, and among all this, she is an incorrigible romantic, falls in love frequently. Even now, my mother has so much energy for everything in life; we don't have that much life spirit. Or, if one thinks from the other side, our times have more limitations. Theirs was the time to break all shackles, to summon the new, the novel. We have crossed that.'

'Fine, you explain well. Now, tell us a little about your family. We'd like to know.'

'All this time, my family meant my mother's house in America, my father's house in Britain, and my grandfather's house in India. My travels were between three residences in three continents. Mine is a global family! My grandfather is still alive. I try to visit him every holiday. Through him and my aunt, my contact with India is so strong, so close. Now, a new bonding has come, my daughter; my personal family has now begun. She is an Indian girl, a Bengali girl. We, mother and daughter, haven't settled down properly yet. She is just three months old. She came to my lap when she was just a month old. I do some writing, make films. I suppose all that will go out of the window for some time.

But I desperately wanted to be a mother. I was getting older, so when would I enjoy motherhood? I had no patience to wait for nine months.'

'Congratulations! Wish you and your daughter the very best. Wish you all the happiness, joy, and success. What is the reaction of your family members about this?'

'Everyone is overjoyed.'

'Great! This creative life, your writing, and then making films, is your inspiration your mother?'

'To talk of inspiration in the early stages of life, to tell the truth, my mother was a busy person, so not from her that much, but I received more inspiration from my father. Because he is not from the world of art and literature, he has great respect for the fields and believes them to be invaluable. Although divorced, he has great respect for my mother's work. For my own work, I am greatly indebted to my father's wife, Eileen. She worked harder to give me more free time for my studies, for my work. Today, the time has come for me to offer unlimited gratitude to my father George Anderson, and my stepmother Eileen. Many thanks to my grandfather in Kolkata, Jyotiprasad Choudhury, and to my aunt and uncle in Delhi, Bidisha and Anubhav Mohapatra. They gave me mental strength at every moment of difficulty. They helped a great deal in the making of this film. And my two little brothers taught me love. My mother Professor Bipasha Anderson need not be thanked separately.'

'Before we end, have you anything to add about your work that wasn't covered by these questions? If anything important has been left out that should be said?'

'Many thanks. You have helped me greatly by asking this question. At the end, let me tell you something that is very important to me. Many times, through many questions, you wanted to hear something that I wasn't able to say.

'No, in my personal life, my mother is not my role model. She is not my inspiration in my professional work either. But, at the basis of making this film is my mother. In every way, my mother. But she doesn't know that. To look at this in another way, perhaps, in my growth as an artist, my mother was indirectly responsible, in a much more active and an important way than a role model. Between the two of us, between mother and daughter, there is no friendship and no enmity, but there is a bond, a deep, integral, unbreakable, innate bond. I have felt it. I hope that my first film will end her long inner restlessness. I believe that my first work will be therapeutic for any unhappiness existing in my mother's life, of any unspoken frustration. My mother is successful everywhere. She is good-looking, writes well, teaches well, dances well, makes love well, and she is a great conversationist. There are only two things where she didn't succeed: first, she couldn't tame her daughter, she totally failed in this; and second, for many years, after several starts, she kept on trying to write a novel. The novel was ready in her mind. But somehow, she could not complete writing it. Failing again and again, finally in a spurt of anger and sorrow over this failure, she burnt her manuscript.

'I firmly hope my first film will completely wipe out the pain of both these failures from my mother's life.'

'But how? Excuse me, I couldn't follow you.'

'Okay. Come to the beginning of the mystery story. Finally losing patience, my mother had thrown all her papers of the novel into the trash can of the incinerator room, so that the janitor puts it into the incinerator. She didn't turn back on it out of great frustration with her wasted effort. Very fortunately, I went into the incinerator room that very evening. I was searching for something in the discarded newspapers. I was extremely shocked to see my mother's sheets of typed work in the wastebasket. My entering that room was purely coincidental. Feeling quite disturbed and scared, I took out the entire file and kept it with me very carefully. That was a file I was familiar with since my childhood. This was an example to show how important and dear someone's work can be. Mother had kept it with her for years, carefully hidden; she never showed it to anyone. She was trying to write a novel in secret. She started afresh several times, didn't give up. Then, suddenly, one day, driven by some frustration that stemmed from an almost suicidal state of mind, she gave up and threw away the file in the incinerator room. In her mind, she had already reduced it to ashes. That was the acceptance of defeat by my arrogant mother.

'The entire matter pained me. I, too, learnt a lesson from this in a vague way. The lesson for an artist was to be totally immersed in art. Then came the acute pain when that involvement broke, followed by the frustration of giving up and of accepting defeat. Slowly, the outer layers peeled off to reveal the core of pain. I was then a teenager. The very restless and disobedient daughter of my mother.

'After that, I read my mother's incomplete novel many times, begun many times and discarded many times, finally uncontrollable, and therefore left to be burnt, the manuscript like an addict. I developed a connection with it after having reading it so many times. In one way, I too, was my mother's uncontrollable disobedient child, given up after many trials.

'The intimacy that grew between me and my mother's manuscript is the basis on which my first film rests. The seed of the story, background, main characters—all have been taken from her manuscript. I have taken the title of the film also from her book—*The Parrot Green Saree*. Widows wear colourless white sarees there. This name was given by my mother. My film came out of my mother's book. But, my mother wasn't sure of what she wanted to write. I definitely don't know that. We never spoke about it. That's why I closed the film in my own way.

'Mother's book described a village where all the women were widows. A student from the city visited the village for secret espionage for a revolutionary political cause. Then, after seeing the helpless desperation of the women of the village, there arose in her mind restlessness, impatience with the anti-humanitarian orders of revolutionary politics, and clash of revolutionary ideals and human values. All these became knotted in a way too complex for her to resolve. She wanted to establish an integral connection with the unfortunate women of the village, but was unable to surrender herself totally to their cause. Her hands were tied, and over her head hung the sword of group politics and revolutionary ideals that made her ineffective.

'I went to the widows' village after nearly thirty years, and asked if any of them remembered my mother. And thus, I became involved anew with their lives.

'The society had changed and new problems were arising; this was a new era. The widows' village too had changed. Making my mother's material the context, I built my own film. My light and air mixed with Mother's earth and water. Instead of regarding this a mother–daughter initiative, bringing together two generations, why not think of it as joining hands of two artists? I am very ashamed that I didn't attempt any discussion with my mother, nor tried to take her permission. Mother has a whimsical poetic temperament. Had she said "no", I couldn't have proceeded. In fact, there is nothing for my mother to be angry or irritated in this.

Her creative work was burnt to ashes ten years back. This film has emerged from those ashes like a phoenix. Now it is no longer her creation; it is our joint creation. I have given my mother's name as the story writer, also without asking for her permission. Mother can file a case about this, of course.

'I have had many quarrels, many misunderstandings with my mother all through my life. This is my olive branch. I have dedicated this film to my small daughter. She was born in that Bidhobagram, widows' village. I have named her Tia (parrot) in Bangla, my mother's tongue.'

As if automatically, Bipasha switched off the laptop. She didn't even remember to take out the CD.

Bipasha sat like a statue. Colours danced under her closed lids, her ears rang with waves of sounds—they surrounded her, encircled her, and turned circles of many colours round her for a long time. Rohini's infancy—her childhood and adolescence—her busy life and career—her vulnerability for love—her resentment—her going away—her going far away—

Bipasha opened her eyes and sat up. Were her eyes burning? The tall glass of ginseng tea was still untouched; the ice cubes had melted. Little Minto curled near her feet like a small ball of wool. She rubbed her feet affectionately on his fur and picked up the glass of iced tea. She needed the drink.

Bipasha saw herself in the long mirror.

No, all her life, she had never missed a golden chance that was offered to her.

A wrong decision should not be allowed to repeat the long, delayed confusion. Bipasha, grab the moment.

She would have to leave for New York tomorrow morning. Somehow. Would there be a seat available in time? Let's check and see. Otherwise, she would start in her car early morning. Bipasha had to go.

Before that, she must write her speech for the banquet and email it to David and Bighnaraje.

Bipasha Anderson got up from the chair, poured herself a small cognac, and returned to her bed. She leaned back and pulled the laptop. There were many things to be done—air ticket, speech, packing. Big occasion, she must dress up for her daughter.

Never before in her life had she felt so complete.

Other Books by the Author in the Series:

In a Foreign Land, By Chance
(*Probashe Daiber Boshe*)

I, Anupam
(*Ami Anupam*)